I told him I was sorry, but we were learning the Distributive Law, and if I didn't use it, I couldn't do my assignment.

I saw his eyes dart to my book. He had no idea what subject this law had to do with. For all he knew, it was social studies or science. All he knew for sure was that it wasn't English. "Look," he said, "I'm an English professor. When you specialize in using your verbal skills, you let your math skills atrophy." He paused. "Atrophy means to wither up."

"Mom's an artist, but she can do math," I said. I was about to suggest that he probably could, too, but he interrupted me.

"I'm sure your mother is superior to me in many ways," he said. He was getting angry.

"That's not what I meant." I hoped I sounded apologetic.

He told me to hand over the book. I pointed out the half of the page where it explained the law. I had a blank sheet of paper. "Look," I said. I drew a rectangle, divided not in equal parts. I labeled one b and one c. I labeled the side a. "So I'm supposed to know that a (b+c) = ab + ac. That's what Mrs. Phipps told us."

"So what?" my father said "Sounds like you get it."

I told him to look at the problems. They said things like "5 (7 + 3) =" and "2 (x + 4) =."

"This is a royal pain in the neck," he said. "I thought you were just coming over here for a quiet evening. You never cause this kind of trouble at home. Other kinds, but not this."

He said "home."

"What?" I asked.

"Have you heard one word I said?" I didn't want to tell him what word I heard, so I nodded. "I don't think so," he said. "You need to pay attention. Maybe you don't pay attention to anybody else, but you need to pay attention to me."

"Okay."

He must have read over that half-page explanation of the Distributive Law four times, but it clearly made no sense to him. Here was a man who thought he could read poems that made no sense to anybody, but when it came to math, he was no better than me.

He slammed the book shut. "What did your goddamn teacher tell you about this?" he asked. "You just have to teach it back to me, and then you'll have it."

NO TAKEBACKS

A NOVEL BY

PATTY FRIEDMANN

Tiny Satchel Press
Philadelphia

Tiny Satchel Press
311 West Seymour Street
Philadelphia, PA 19144
tinysatchelpress@gmail.com
www.tinysatchelpress.com

Distributed by
Bella Books
P.O. Box 10543
Tallahassee, FL 32302
1-800-729-4992

Tiny Satchel Press Publisher: Victoria A. Brownworth
Art director/cover concept: Maddy Gold
Cover design: Christopher Bauer
Cover production: Jennifer Mercer
Book design: Stacia Seaman
Tiny Satchel Press logo: Chris Angelucci

Printed in the United States of America.
First edition.
ISBN 978-0-9849146-3-0

For Carmine, Kennedy, and Summer with all my love, Omie

CHAPTER ONE

I was just waiting to see what Samantha Rivers was going to do. She played that drama card to get attention at least once a year, and this definitely was the time she was going to play it. All the other people in the class kind of rolled their eyes every time because they'd heard it before, but it felt personal to me. I felt like she should keep her mouth shut, the way I did.

Mrs. Phipps had said that for the Thanksgiving program the seventh grade was going to do a presentation about how our ancestors had come to America. Ancestors! That was a subject just ripe for picking for Samantha. The words weren't out of Mrs. Phipps's mouth before Samantha's hand was in the air.

Mrs. Phipps called on her. Poor Mrs. Phipps was almost the only person in the room who didn't know what was coming. Except for Aiden and some girl named Emily, who'd both transferred into St. Michael's this year. "Yes, Samantha?" Mrs. Phipps said.

"Well, see, like, I don't have any ancestors," Samantha said.

"Everybody has ancestors," Mrs. Phipps said. "Maybe you..."

This was just what Samantha wanted. "What I mean

is, I don't know who my real ancestors are. See, I'm adopted."

Mrs. Phipps was quiet for a few seconds. I actually think Samantha was the first student who'd ever brought up this subject in relation to ancestors. Mrs. Phipps had been at St. Michael's since I started in pre-K, and she looked kind of old when I got there, so it was hard to believe that not knowing who your ancestors were when you're adopted never crossed her mind. But I figured maybe it never came up before.

Maybe most adopted kids were like me.

Maybe you let people know once that you were adopted, and then you just dropped the subject and worked around it. No big deal. If you had to do something about your ancestors, you asked your mother who her ancestors were. I wouldn't ask my father, but that's another story.

Mrs. Phipps made her face look very serious, which by then she should have known didn't trick kids in seventh grade. We knew she was stalling for time. Finally, she said, "You know, Samantha is actually raising an interesting question. Who are your real ancestors if you're adopted?"

Naturally, a lot of my friends turned and looked at me. That's what friends were for, to make a person nervous in class. I could feel enough attention turning in my direction that Mrs. Phipps picked up on it, and I started turning red. I think I was more angry than embarrassed, but being angry and embarrassed felt pretty much the same right then.

"Otto?" she asked.

If everybody thought I was going to get up there

and start an "I'm more adopted than you" contest with Samantha, they were going to have to be disappointed.

"Seems to me," I said, "that if you're adopted you just claim the grandparents and great-grandparents and stuff that you can know about, which are the ones your parents give you when they adopt you." The room was dead silent. Everybody actually was interested. "I mean, if the adoption agency or whatever told your parents that you're half German-Jewish and half Irish-Catholic, what good will that do you if you're supposed to be in a play about your ancestors? You don't know if they came over when you were born or on the Mayflower or whatever."

I knew those facts about myself, the German-Jewish and Irish-Catholic facts, I mean.

People started laughing.

Samantha didn't even raise her hand. "There weren't any Irish Catholics on the Mayflower," she said. "And there sure weren't any *Jews*."

Now I was sorry I'd opened my mouth. Social studies was one of the subjects I got terrible grades in, and everybody knew it. Especially Samantha. I had this feeling that Samantha thought her parents lucked out and my parents got screwed. The way her mother paraded around school, I knew she definitely felt she lucked out.

Mrs. Phipps saved me. Teachers at St. Michael's were kind that way. St. Michael's is an Episcopal school, but everybody goes there.

"Now you guys know perfectly well what Otto means," Mrs. Phipps said. "I want each of you to find a person in your family tree who you can put in our play. You can't just make up a person if all you know is where that person came from."

I had to admit, I liked Mrs. Phipps pretty much. At our school, I was in what my mother called the "Adderall for lunch bunch." St. Michael's made sure each class had one-quarter kids with learning problems, one-quarter gifted, and one-half regular. My father made sure to tell me that kids who went to the office at noon for Adderall were not in the gifted program. Mrs. Phipps had been at the school long enough, it seemed to me, to think kids like me were all right.

Samantha probably didn't like Mrs. Phipps for that reason. And she wasn't going to let her get away with anything. "It seems to me," Samantha said without raising her hand, "that I could *make up* an ancestor just as well as make up a story about one who's not even really my relative. I mean, I know my birth mother was pure English. Probably her ancestors *did* come over on the Mayflower."

Yeah, and they were really proud when your birth mother got pregnant and gave the baby away, I wanted to say.

"If that's what you'd like to do," Mrs. Phipps said, "I think it would be a lovely addition to our program." She looked at me. She understood without even asking that I was adopted. "What about you, Otto?"

"I guess I'll ask my mom."

That felt good to say.

In any other place besides New Orleans, people could have walked or ridden their bikes to school by seventh grade. Actually, the poor black kids probably started taking the bus in elementary school. But kids who went to St. Michael's were all rich and spoiled, and absolutely everybody rode in carpools until they graduated in eighth grade. I figured their parents had invested so much money in tuition and braces that they weren't going to risk their kids getting hit by a car. And the truth of the matter was that most of us probably could have gotten hit by a car because we had so little experience getting around the city on our own. I liked to skateboard, and so did a bunch of my friends, so we'd learned to be a little smart on the streets, but we were the exception. Anyway, I rode in carpool, and that day it wasn't my mother's turn to drive.

So there was no way to talk to her about the Thanksgiving play before I got home. I'd been figuring I'd catch her before my father showed up. I needed to brainstorm ideas so I could have something to say in school the next day. I wasn't the world's greatest when it came to getting my homework assignments done, but I had something on the line here. I was going to walk into school tomorrow and have an interesting story that would make Samantha's make-believe Pilgrim ancestor as ghostly as Samantha. Samantha had white-blond hair and very pale skin, though she had brown eyes. She said she was French blond, which was a little weird, given that she was supposed to be pure English. From everything I'd seen on reality TV, people who had blond hair and brown eyes were kind of white trash and did car repo and got really fat when they grew up.

When Mrs. Eugene pulled up to the curb at my house, I saw my father's car in the driveway. I was so disappointed, I almost forgot to say thank you. But carpool mothers didn't expect much anyway. I ran to the house, maybe hoping if I was fast enough I'd get to my mother before my father did. I wanted to be alone with her.

I hoped I could catch her in her studio. My mother was sort of a famous artist in New Orleans who made vases and bowls and pots and sold them for a lot more money than you'd think people would pay for those things. But she said they were decorative. We just never had any in our house. I thought maybe she'd be alone, maybe glazing. I liked it best when she used the pottery wheel.

No such luck. She was in the kitchen. And he was standing there, watching her cut bell peppers to stuff for dinner. My father liked stuffed bell peppers. He liked beef any way you cooked it. When I tried to be a vegetarian when I was nine, he laughed at me. I ate around the meat until I was nearly starving, then finally gave up.

"How come you're home?" I asked him.

"Veterans' Day," he said. "Tulane lets those kids take so many days off I can't believe their parents pay tuition. Last month it was Jewish holidays nobody's ever heard of."

Half the time my father called the school *Jew-lane*. And those holidays? My mother is half Jewish, the half that counted according to Jewish law, she told me. We didn't celebrate those holidays, but I sure knew about Rosh Hashanah and Yom Kippur. I'd learned about them from kids at school. The gifted program was loaded with Jewish kids. Next year they were all going to have Bar Mitzvahs. The Jewish boys were sure by then we were going to want to dance with the girls. I thought first we were going to have to quit fighting with them the way we'd been fighting with them since pre-K.

My mother asked me if I was hungry. I'm always hungry.

"He needs to get to his homework," my father said.

"Actually, I need to talk to Mom as part of my homework," I said.

My father looked at my mother funny, as if he was asking her if this had ever happened before or if I was just trying to get out of something, as usual. So my mother started rinsing the pepper off her hands. But she was looking at me as if to say, *C'mon, Otto, show him that you're not goofing off.*

I looked straight at my father. "The class is doing a school play for Thanksgiving, and each of us has to be one of our ancestors."

I'd hoped not to tell him, because I didn't want any Fisher ancestors, but I had to, now.

He didn't hesitate. "You don't have any ancestors. You're adopted."

I couldn't believe how much that hurt my feelings. But I wouldn't let tears come into my eyes. I'd practiced for a long time not letting him get to me.

"We talked about ancestors in class," I said. "And if you're adopted, either you can talk about what you know about your birth parents, or you can just say that your actual parents have given you your grandparents and great-grandparents and all up the line."

"Technically, your actual parents are your *birth* parents," my father said.

"David," my mother said, "don't play semantics with the child."

I didn't know what semantics were, but I could tell she meant he was picking my words apart for no reason. That was something he was really good at.

My father turned to me. "Discuss this with your mother." He picked up the mail that was sitting on the kitchen counter and walked out of the room.

I still didn't let any tears fall. It wouldn't do my mother any good to see me sad.

"Well!" she said. "I think we can find some really good ancestors right in my family. I mean, even ancestors that I knew almost directly."

I told her what Samantha was doing with the stupid Mayflower.

"Do you want to walk around school all day in a Pilgrim costume?" she asked, and I smiled. And then she told me about her grandfather who had died in Auschwitz. He had lived in Poland before World War II and had been gassed in the biggest concentration camp. I wasn't smiling, but I was feeling like I definitely belonged to her family. After all, my parents had adopted me from the Jewish agency because my mother could claim Jewish origins.

I wrote an entire page for homework. Triple-spaced, but that was okay. We learned keyboarding in fifth grade, but I didn't have my own computer, so I had to use the one in the family room. Ada helped me a lot. I didn't know what I was going to do next year when she left for college. The computer was the least of it. Ada loved me like I was *her* baby. Her name was pronounced Ah-duh. "Like in Nabokov," she would tell new people, and they would look at her like she was nuts. My father had named her, and he had said, "We'll send her to a school where everybody will have read Nabokov." Every year Ada laughed because she was at Newman School, the fanciest school in the city for smart kids, and her new teachers called her Ay-duh.

"For my Thanksgiving person, I am going to be Shebsel Silber. He was my great-grandfather. He was born in Poland in a small city called Vilna in 1880. He was sort of rich because he had a shoe factory. Which wasn't good after a while, because he was Jewish. When Hitler took over in Germany, he hated the Jews. Hitler really blamed the rich Jews for everything that was wrong, so he put them in concentration camps. And the first thing Hitler did when he went to war was to declare war on Poland.

"My great-grandfather was really smart. He was afraid his family might be in danger. So he sent his wife and children to America. One of his children was my grandmother, who I know, but she's old. That explains why she's not dead, even though her father got killed. Hitler rounded up all the Jews in Poland. The worst place to go was Auschwitz, which you pronounce *Owshwitz*. They would make you walk into this room. You would think you were taking a shower. But really you were being given this gas called Zyklon B that killed you. Then they burned your body. But if you had gold teeth or something, they took those first, before they burned your body. Then they buried you in a pit.

"I'm going to be Shebsel Silber. He was very kind to his kids. And he gave a lot of money to poor people. But he got killed by the Nazis because they hated Jews. My mother is alive because he saved her life."

I thought it was the best thing I'd ever written.

My mother had sat down with me and helped me with every sentence, written in pencil, before I put it on the computer. Then Ada checked it over before I printed it. I went into the living room waving it, so excited to show it to my mother. The TV was on. I didn't notice that there wasn't a commercial running. What can I say? With ADHD, it's hard to pay attention to everything. Really, it's hard to pay attention to anything.

"I know I'm going to get an A," I said.

"Sh!" my father said, not letting the sound come out for more than a fraction of a second, so he wouldn't miss whatever was so important on TV. I looked at the screen. It was one of those guys on FOX News. Their shows played over and over, all day. And they filled up time saying the same thing different ways. At least that's what my mother said once. I knew she disagreed with their politics. And that meant she tried her best not to listen and get annoyed. Most of the time, she read magazines in front of the TV. We had only two TV sets in our house. And the other one, in Ada's room, only came when Ada paid for it. She had cable in her room because she paid for that, too. Ada was probably the only person in the history of Newman School who worked checkout at Winn-Dixie.

My mother reached out her hand to take the paper from me, not saying a word. Her eyes got kind of teary while she read. "This is wonderful," she said. "David, you have to read this."

"Sh!" my father said.

I took the paper from my mother and went back to my room.

Each of us went up to Mrs. Phipps's desk with our papers. After she read mine, Mrs. Phipps looked up at me, and I knew the expression on her face said, *I think this is too good for you to have written, Otto, but I'm not going to say it.* So I said, "I talked to my mom a lot last night, and every time she told me something, she helped me write it down."

"This is very good," Mrs. Phipps said. She looked actually kind of sad. She'd already read most of the class's papers, even though I was close to the front of the alphabet. Fisher. Without a "c," my father reminded me. I never understood why he pointed that out a lot of the time, but he said one day I'd be glad it was just regular Fisher. People whose name was Fischer got looked at differently. Anyway, Mrs. Phipps hadn't looked sad about anyone else's paper. She hadn't looked like she had any kind of feelings at all about anybody else's paper.

While I was still up at her desk, she said to the class, "Otto's got an ancestor I think we need to talk about."

I knew it. Samantha raised her hand.

Mrs. Phipps ignored her. Well, sort of. She looked right at Samantha and said, "No, Samantha, this is not someone that he thinks might be his biological ancestor. This is his mother's grandfather."

"But..." Samantha said.

This time Mrs. Phipps did ignore her. "Otto's great-grandfather died in a concentration camp when the Nazis were killing Jews during World War II. So I think..."

Samantha's hand shot right up, but she didn't wait to

be called on. "So if he got killed, how can Otto be alive? Well, I mean, I know how Otto can be alive, because this guy isn't his actual ancestor, but how can his mom be alive?"

I would have wanted to punch Samantha, except that I knew Mrs. Phipps would explain how my grandmother escaped and was saved, and then my mother was born, and the end, *so there, Samantha.*

My story of Shebsel Silber was going to be the opening story of the play, and I was going to have to learn a lot of lines.

I went to resource three times a week. Usually, we worked on reading, but for two weeks straight we did nothing but practice my lines. It is very hard to learn lines with ADHD. When I was a Cub Scout, I had to go to resource just to learn the motto. My father was so embarrassed at the second scout meeting that he made my mother go after that. I never entered the oratory competition. That drove my father crazy, too, since he is in the English Department at Tulane. He made Ada memorize poetry from the time she was three. And not nursery rhymes, either. She told me that he laughed at her the first—and only—time she brought home a Judy Blume book. He expected her to read somebody called Dickens. My only way to get around that was just not to read at all.

My father refused to let me borrow any of his clothes for my costume. My mother figured that an old shirt and some pants that were baggy on me would look old-fashioned if I wore suspenders. She could buy me a hat, and I'd look like somebody who lived in 1939. She even found silver hair spray left over from Halloween at Walgreens. But my father wouldn't let me touch his clothes. He said I'd ruin them, so my mother and I went to the Salvation Army, and that was better because I wouldn't have to worry. I knew my lines. I went to school on the Monday before Thanksgiving. My mother even promised she'd bring my father to see the play. "Theater is an adjunct of literature," she said to me. "That's what I'm going to tell him."

I was so nervous I was shaking like our dog used to when we took him to the vet. You couldn't see it unless you touched me. Everybody in the whole school showed up for assemblies, the pre-K kids all the way up to the eighth grade. That meant all the grown-ups would have nothing else to do, and nobody took a break at St. Michael's because, really, they were there for us, so people like Coach Jorge, and Mrs. Banks in the office, the nice one who had all the Adderall in her drawer, all were in the audience. And of course, all the seventh-grade parents. I'd been there since pre-K, and they all knew me. Well, the boy parents knew me as a good person, and the girl parents probably knew me as somebody their daughters complained about. Except Katie's and Anne's mothers. We were three of six kids who'd been at St. Michael's for pre-K, and when you're in pre-K, boys and girls go over to each other's houses. Katie's and Anne's mothers liked me.

From the side of the stage I found my mother in the audience. She was wearing a very pink shirt. She told me before I left for school that she was wearing it so I could find her. Right away I checked to see if my father was with her. He promised while I was eating breakfast that he'd come. "Your dad doesn't have any classes on Monday mornings," my mother had said, "so of course he'll be there."

"I've got a stack of papers this high to grade before the little bastards come back from break," he said, and he held his hands a foot apart. "College kids don't get away with turning in one sheet of paper."

Ada was at the table. "My English teacher said that the shorter a piece is, the harder it is," she said. "That's why novels are easier than short stories, and poems are hardest of all."

"Your teacher needs her ass kicked," my father said. But I could see he was thinking, like maybe there was some truth in what Ada said.

There was an empty seat next to my mother. That was pretty good, considering she was in the third row. Saving seats wasn't allowed for kids, but parents let each other do it. I kept poking my head out, but my father didn't walk in until I was already on the stage, saying my part.

"My name is Shebsel Silber. I'm the only ancestor today who never lived in America. But there's a reason for it, and it's a sad reason." That's when my father walked in. I almost lost my place, but I didn't. By the time I finished my speech, the room was completely silent. Even the little pre-K kids weren't wiggling. Nobody clapped for a few seconds, and then my mother started clapping, and everybody else did, too. I looked at my father. He was very pale, and he wasn't clapping. I noticed he clapped when Samantha did her two lines about being Jane

Worthington at Plymouth Rock. She had on a genuine Pilgrim costume, and I could feel my friends' eyes rolling around so much the audience could see them. Anybody who wanted to could look it up and see there was no such person. My friend Ren said so.

After the play was over, all the seventh-grade kids and their parents got to stay in the auditorium for a little reception that the room mothers set up. It was pretty nice. There were even some sandwiches with the crusts cut off. My father piled his plate up. There were roast beef and turkey sandwiches, and they were free, and that was worth showing up for, at least judging from how pleased he looked while he was standing at the refreshments table. I looked around to make sure the other kids weren't noticing that my father was being a pig. He wasn't hugely fat, but he was kind of shaped like a pear. If he didn't wear a jacket, you could see that he had very narrow shoulders and no chest, really, but his belly poked out, and he had big, fat hips. My grandmother in South Carolina, who was his mother, said he had a body like a girl. She was pretty mean.

I went over to the table to get myself a sandwich and ask what he thought of the play. I picked up a tuna-salad sandwich. "You ought to put that on a plate, Otto," he said.

"I'm going to put it right into my mouth," I said.

"Then at least use a napkin."

A napkin actually wasn't a bad idea. The tuna was kind of oozing out of the sandwich.

"You like the play?" I asked.

"You did a good job."

"The very beginning was probably the best part,"

I said. It wasn't smart to say that, because I was only trying to let him know that I saw him come in late, but I couldn't stop myself.

"I'm just saying you did your lines very well."

"Okay."

I went off to hang with my friends, but until my parents left it wasn't going to feel like real school again. I knew where they were the entire time they stayed, even if they didn't pay attention to where I was. And that's why I could hear them talking.

"You didn't even clap," my mother was saying,

"It wasn't exactly the end of a scene or anything," my father said.

"But it was our kid, for God's sake. And he did a good job."

That felt really good. My mother said nice things to me all the time, but I knew she was the kind of mother who believed in making kids have good self-esteem. For her to say it behind my back meant she was being honest.

"I told the kid he did a good job," my father said. "He was over at the food table. Naturally. And naturally, he was eating like it was a trough. He wouldn't know a plate if you hit him over the head with one. I hate to think what other parents thought. Probably that we're raising a little heathen."

"Look around this room and tell me if you see one kid with a plate."

I was glad I was behind a bookcase where they couldn't see me. The library doubled for an auditorium.

"You're missing the point," my father said, and he sounded as angry with my mother as he usually did with me. I hoped nobody else was listening. "The kid definitely learned his lines. No embarrassment there. Now why you had to put him in front of everybody with that sob story and all that Jewish foolishness is beyond me. This is an Episcopal school. His name is Fisher. F-i-s-h-e-r. No 'c' in there. Not Jewish."

"Probably a fifth of the kids here are Jewish," my mother said.

"Well, we're not."

My mother looked around to be sure no one was paying attention to them. Her voice got lower, but I still could hear her. "We told them we'd raise the baby Jewish. I know we lied, but we don't have to be so in-your-face about it. Don't forget he was named in the synagogue in front of a lot of people."

"You can wave your hands over him and say he's a robin redbreast, but that doesn't make him one." That was one of my father's South Carolina sayings. He might have had a PhD in English, but he sometimes pulled out some dumb expressions.

Ren, who *was* Jewish, came by just then. I told him I was eavesdropping on my parents. I didn't need to tell him to go away. He wasn't interested in eavesdropping on parents. Thank goodness.

"Well, if David Duke ever comes back and starts lining up the Jews on the levee, Otto's going to be on somebody's list," my mother said.

"And I'll say I don't know him."

"We made a deal," my mother said, then turned and walked away. She was looking for me.

CHAPTER TWO

Ada was late for dinner that night. She hung out at her boyfriend Finn's house after school a lot of afternoons when she didn't have a shift at Winn-Dixie, and he dropped her off. Finn was cool. He was the center on the basketball team because he was tall. Otherwise he didn't care about sports. He liked playing tennis with his father on Saturdays because they talked. He always talked to me, too, even though we had nothing to talk about. He wasn't even really interested in the Saints, Ada told me, but he paid attention a little, just for me.

Ada slipped right into her seat at the table. It was cold outside, and she was kind of pink and happy looking. "Sorry," she said. She said it like a person who figured she'd be forgiven.

My father shrugged his shoulders. He didn't care where Ada had been. As long as he could say she went to Newman, he was happy. Even though he always told my mother he wanted her in public school. To the outside world, Newman meant she was smart, and he was rich. He wanted her to go to Tulane, even though Ada thought it would mean the exact opposite.

"How'd it go, Starshine?" Ada asked me.

For a second I didn't know what she was talking

about. I guess I'd kind of given myself a rule of forgetting the school play as soon as I got home, so there wouldn't be any fighting. I could tell my parents didn't like the subject. Then I remembered. It was the big thing about me.

"Your brother didn't forget any of his lines," my father said.

"There wasn't a dry eye in the house," my mother said.

I looked with just my eyes in my father's direction. This was what I was afraid of.

"She's exaggerating. Your brother did get up there with some histrionics, but I think that saying he brought the audience to tears is a little much."

I didn't know what histrionics meant, but the way it came out of my father, it sounded like an insult. Saying something bad about a sad story of an old man being murdered wasn't fair.

"Hey," I said. "It wasn't histrionics. It was really sad."

My father started to laugh. The only time he laughed was when only the family was around and he was making fun of one of us. "I'll give you twenty dollars if you can tell me what histrionics means," he said to me.

"Otto knows very well it means acting phony, don't you, Otto?" Ada said. I nodded. "So, pay up," she said to my father. She was joking around, and I laughed.

"Listen, Miss Newman Senior," my father said, "you were late to dinner as it is. Either you leave this table, or I will."

Ada looked at my mother. The look between them wasn't one of power at all—it was one of fear. All my life,

I'd known that we didn't want my father to leave the room or leave the house. Because then we'd have to wait for him to come back. Ada always told me that when she was small, she was sure he was going to come back in the night and kill her. Ada got up from the table.

"I'll bring you something to eat later," my mother said.

"No, you won't," my father said.

"I ate at Finn's," Ada said in a whisper only my mother and I could hear.

"What did you say?" my father asked.

"Nothing," Ada said, and she left the dining room looking as sad as she probably figured he wanted her to look.

Technically, I was the good kid in the house that night. At least I kind of felt that way. So while my father was reading the *Times-Picayune* after dinner, I decided it was the best time to ask him. He always said that the paper wasn't worth the ink used to print it. He said the only reason he read it was so he could clip out typos to show to his colleagues in the English Department. He'd found a grammar mistake from the Associated Press the day before, and my mother said you'd have thought he'd won the Pulitzer Prize. Anyway, to me that meant that he could be interrupted. It wasn't like during Bill O'Reilly or something on TV where a sentence would go by and he could never go back to it. Even if Bill O'Reilly was going to say it a different way in a few minutes.

I had to ask him about Coach Jorge's basketball

system. I had the flyer to give him. "You want to read this, or should I tell you about it?" I asked.

"Whatever you prefer," he said.

"Well," I said, holding out the paper, "It's like this. Coach Jorge thought I did real good this morning." My father frowned. "Real well. Really well. Very well. Anyway, for basketball, he needs the dads to volunteer taking turns as assistant coaches. So this is a sign-up." I pushed the sheet at him. The explanation was at the top. A place to sign up was in the middle of the page. My father looked at it, then laid it flat on his lap.

"Was there even any point in showing me this?" he asked.

I knew he was thinking that he just wouldn't do it, no matter what. But I was going to pretend I thought things might change. "You get to pick the hour and day," I said. "And there are so many dads that you only have to do it twice. That's only two hours, total. You wouldn't even have to come to games. Mom can come to games. Or Ada. Or nobody."

He was quiet for many seconds. He let me just stand there. "Son, do you ever pay attention?" He looked at me, waited for me to look him in the eye. I nodded. "What makes you think I've made any philosophical changes?"

"Sometimes people do change their minds about things," I said, but my voice was weak.

"Well, I'm a man of my convictions, and one thing that I always will find useless is sports. Not only do I think that competitive sports is socially unacceptable, I feel it is the bane of the school environment. Do you follow me?"

I hated when he used complicated language when a simple sentence would do.

"What I'm trying to say is that I hate sports, and I think sports has no place in schools. It has no place in a school like St. Michael's, and it's the ruination of a school like Tulane. You have no idea how much money is drained from academic necessities like my department because of football and basketball."

"But I'm good at basketball," I said.

"And if you came home after school and did homework instead of playing basketball, you wouldn't say things such as 'I did real good.'"

I was going to cry if I didn't get angry right then. "I'm not Ada, you know. If you wanted a kid like you, you should've had another one."

My mother walked into the living room right then. My father said to her, "tell this kid he better get out of here if he knows what's good for him."

My mother picked up the flyer from my father's lap. "Can moms volunteer?" she asked.

"No!" I said, and I ran off to my room.

It was hard finding a way to get to school early because I was in a carpool. Finally, I begged my mother to get me out just this one time, and Ada got Finn to drop me off on their way to Newman. It was a little out of their way, but they didn't care. Ada was almost six years older than I was, and I was sort of her baby. She told me once how she said to the social worker that she had head lice and the house was full of cockroaches when the lady was coming to inspect to see if her family was a good one to adopt a baby. She heard the lady tell our mother that Ada was just jealous of a new sibling. "I was trying to make them give the baby to a better family," Ada told me, "but how could I come out and say that?"

I needed to see Coach Jorge before school started. He was in his little office next to the gym when I walked in. "Hey, kid, you should be in class," he said.

I told him I'd come early to talk to him.

Coach put aside the paper he was working on. He was the kind of guy who liked kids to come talk to him. "You did good yesterday in the play," he said.

"Thanks," I said. Coach was allowed to use bad English. English wasn't the language he was born speaking, and besides, people in sports weren't snotty about stuff like that. In fact, if you listened to sportscasters on TV, they almost went out of their way to talk bad. Badly?

"You're good on the court, too," he said.

"That's what I need to talk to you about," I said. He leaned forward a little. I thought he could tell from the way I said it that I wasn't there with good news. "My dad won't sign the paper." I handed him the flyer I took home the day before. I'd tried not to get it too messed up, but in my backpack papers somehow always got folded. I smoothed it out. Coach just waved it away anyway.

"I forget where your dad works," Coach said. "He's a doctor, right?"

I felt myself getting a little embarrassed. My father had a PhD in English, so he walked around insisting that people call him Dr. Fisher. Of course, the headmaster of our school had a doctorate in education, which my father said was the square root of shit, and he insisted on being called "doctor," too. My mother said that at her college in Massachusetts, everybody on the faculty had a doctorate, but they were all called Mr. or Mrs. or Ms. If you wanted Dr. Somebody, you went to the infirmary. That didn't bother my father at all. At St. Michael's, he was Dr. Fisher.

"My father teaches English at Tulane," I said. "That means, like, I think, maybe sixteen hours a week."

Coach understood right away. "He could do it?"

"But he hates sports," I said.

Coach actually smiled. "You know, I've been at this school, what, twelve years? And I never met a daddy didn't like sports. I mean, some daddies, oh, they were terrible, couldn't make a one-point shot if you gave them all day. And a lot of daddies, they holler way too much. That's a big problem." He smiled at me, trying to make me feel better. He whispered. "But mamas, they holler more." I smiled back. I knew a lot of mothers like that. I also knew mine wasn't one of them. "Why your daddy doesn't like sports?"

That was a better question than I realized. "My father says it's because sports takes too much money from the budget for English at Tulane," I said. As soon as the words came out of my mouth, they sounded stupid. One of the main reasons they sounded stupid, which Coach had no way of knowing, was that my father hated the English Department almost as much as he hated the football team. They fought all the time in the English Department. My mother said that was the way it was in every department in every university in the country, and I should pay no attention. But it felt weird when my parents invited other professors to dinner, and I'd heard my father the previous month grumbling about how the wife was some kind of moron, trying to expand the focus on the nineteenth century. Who could get worked up over the nineteenth century? I really didn't even care about the twentieth century, and I was born in it.

"So your father didn't always hate sports?" Coach asked.

"What?"

"Your father hates sports because of his job now. Maybe you could remind him of what it felt like when he was thirteen?"

I tried to imagine him at thirteen, and of course the only things I knew about him at thirteen came from Grandmama Fisher. She liked to pick the worst things about people and talk about them, and she could make them very funny. There's nothing worse about a person than being thirteen. I knew that. Last time Grandmama saw me, she was impressed. "Almost forgot you was adopted," she said. My father heard her, but knew better than to correct her English. His PhD pretty much corrected her English for life. "You're good looking," she said to me, "can't see any Jew in you hardly at all. It's like you take after my side, not like your daddy, who takes after Granddaddy's side, shaped like a big fat winter squash. Should've seen him when he was your age. The law of gravity alone kept him off the basketball team." I'd giggled before my father had given me a dirty look.

"He sucked at sports when he was my age," I said.

"Okay," Coach said. He didn't need to say anything more.

I shrugged my shoulders. I figured this meant that I was going to be the first kid not to play after-school basketball because my father refused to help coach. Though I knew there had to have been kids before me whose fathers were dead. Maybe they'd just been too sad to play basketball.

"This isn't the first time this has happened," Coach said. "I mean, this isn't the first time a boy hasn't been able to get his dad to volunteer."

"Oh?"

"There are some fathers who want to take extra turns. They'll be substitute dads for guys like you."

I broke into a big smile. All I could picture was me with a father sub who was really excited about basketball. That was all I could picture. I could forget my regular father really fast. That was the word for him. *Regular* father.

Coach said he thought Ren's father would be a perfect match. He knew Ren and I were friends. Dr. Klinger was a psychiatrist out in Metairie. A real doctor. When I spent the night, he sometimes would go running to the hospital at three a.m. when we were still up goofing around. And, Dr. Klinger had good shoulders.

Ada had a lot of secrets, and I knew some of them. She knew that I knew sometimes, because I'd see her and Finn smoking cigarettes in his car. At least they looked like cigarettes. I was pretty sure they were cigarettes, because it was one thing to get in trouble in the front of the house with our mother, but it was a whole different thing to get in trouble with the police, who sometimes whooshed down our street. Anyway, I just figured out from watching Ada that, the older I got, the more I was going to learn how to hide stuff from our parents.

I probably could have told my mother about basketball, but she always was so nervous about my father getting angry at her that she might have told him. Actually, the word I guess I should use is that she was scared of him. She never came out and said it, but I could tell from the way she backed down all the time. One time we had this guy from the History Department over, and he'd just bought a house. He was saying he'd paid $300,000, and my mother said, "Wow, we paid $150,000 for this one," which was true and made sense, and even I knew it was because we'd lived there forever, but afterward my father had hollered at her all night because she'd made the man feel bad, and how was he ever going to make friends in the departments where everyone was truly erudite, whatever that meant.

So I told my mother when I got home that there was a theater club I'd joined, and would she pick me up late on Tuesdays and Thursdays? She was happy with that, and I was busy thinking about what clothes I'd need for basketball. Everything went well that evening. Just as long as it took for Dr. Klinger to call right after dinner. And for my father to answer the phone.

Dinner had been great. "Otto's signed up for theater," my mother had said, and my father had stopped eating, looking at me like I was a new Otto. I almost wished I had signed up for it. But the only boy I knew who was interested in doing plays was in the eighth grade, and everybody knew he was going to be gay. St. Michael's was a very kind school, mostly because so many of us were screwed up, so being gay wasn't anything you'd get picked on for. In fact nobody got picked on. But that didn't mean I was going to go out for theater. It didn't interest me. Just for starts, if I was going to act, I'd have to memorize lines. And I sucked at memorizing anything. But for right then, it sure felt good for my father to be interested in me.

"Yeah, I really liked being on the stage," I said.

It probably was the wrong thing to say, but my father actually let it slide. "You know, good actors have to understand what their lines mean," my father said.

"I knew that when we did our play yesterday," I said.

"Well, let's not go into that," my father said. He was still being nice. I wondered why he hated poor dead Shebsel. I knew Grandmama hated Jews. She had ways of not saying it outright. Her way of complimenting me, after all, was to announce that I was good looking with hardly a trace of Jew in me. Grandmama Fisher said, *I'm gonna slap you into the middle of next week,* for nothing all the time. She'd smacked my butt and my hand, hard, but so far I'd stayed on the right side with her. I wasn't taking any chances with her son.

"Anyway, I like having an effect on people," I said. "I mean, when I act."

"There are some fine plays out there," my father said.

"I think we're doing..." I stopped. I knew the drama club was doing *Grease.* I didn't know much, but I knew that the Tulane English Department never studied *Grease* for anything. And probably the Theater Department didn't, either. "I think it's a musical," I said.

My mother jumped in. "That's terrific. Singing is a good way to memorize."

The phone rang while my father was interruptible after dinner. But not that interruptible. When my mother hollered from the kitchen, "Can you get that?" he put down the paper. It was only fair; her hands were all covered with glop from washing dishes with no help. I was as guilty as my father. I was leaning against the counter talking to her while she worked. Of course, Ada wasn't even around. But she had an excuse. She was in her room doing her homework. And she probably was. Ada was hell-bent on getting out of town, and if she didn't make a lot of As she was going to be stuck at Tulane, living in that house.

I could hear my father from the kitchen. The house had a lot of open space between rooms, but he also was pretty loud. "Are you serious?" he was saying. "Nobody told me about this." It got quiet for about half a minute. Then, "Look, you know Otto. The kid's a congenital liar. That's a pile of bullshit. Thanks for your charity, but no thanks." I could hear the phone slam from all the way in the kitchen.

When my father came into the kitchen, his face was so red that it made his eyes pop out so you could see the white all the way around the blue. He had his fists up in front of him. I was taller than my mother, but I hid behind her.

"I guess you know who that was," he said to my mother. She shrugged. He looked at me. "Did you lie to your mother, too?" I shrugged. "Don't lie to me now!" he said.

"I told her I was in the theater club, too," I said. I'd seen him shake my mother two times. I'd thought he was going to break her neck.

He looked at my mother. "He lied to both of us," he said. I guess he thought my mother was going to turn around and look at me angrily, but she didn't move. "You know who that was?" he asked her. My mother just barely moved her head, side to side, *no*. "That was Dr. Klinger. You know who he is?"

"That's Ren's dad," I whispered to my mother. I was a little relieved. He'd hollered at Ren's dad, not at Coach Jorge. Dr. Klinger was the nicest dad in the world. Ren's mom was a doctor, too. She specialized in lungs, but I forget what you call that kind of doctor. I didn't know why, but being that kind of doctor made her all snooty, like a know-it-all. She was always pushing Ren off on the housekeeper, but Ren's dad always showed up for everything. Maybe because he was a psychiatrist and understood what was good for people. I figured he could listen to my father and figure out he was a little crazy and not take it personally.

"You know what this little jerk did? He signed up for basketball and acted like some kind of orphan who needed a surrogate father to coach. I bet it's on the days you said you go to drama club, right?"

I nodded.

He kept talking at my mother, even though he was talking to me. "So this doctor, who's a psychiatrist and therefore probably thinks I'm certifiable, gets told Otto needs him to fill in for me. Like he's some poor little black boy that the nice Jewish doctor can mentor and save himself from hell or something."

"Jews don't believe in hell," my mother said.

"Well, neither do I," he said. "And I'm sure no self-respecting Freudian does, either."

"What's a Freudian?" I whispered to my mother. I already was in so much trouble that it didn't make any difference.

"Some psychiatrists practice the way this doctor did back in the 1800s," she whispered back.

"Will you two cut the crap?!" my father said, and he made a step in our direction. I felt my mother back into me.

I knew the best thing to do was apologize. That's what Ada usually did. It made her miserable, but Ada was the one who got hit the least. I didn't feel like apologizing. All I wanted was to play basketball. Just like every other kid. Lots of other kids did worse than me in school. Lots did better. Especially Ren. But, hey, even if Ren grew up to be a doctor, he wasn't going to get as rich as an NBA player. "I just want to play basketball," I said. "You can get rich in the NBA."

My father took another step in our direction. My mother got really tensed up. "Don't touch him," she said.

"Basketball!" he said. "Do you realize what this kid did to me over a stupid game where everybody runs around in their underwear throwing balls at a trash basket over their heads?" I wanted to smile, but I knew he wasn't trying to be funny. "Oh, no, it was your idea to put these kids is fancy schools." He was looking at my mother. In my entire life, he'd never called her by name.

Her name was Elise, but I'd never heard him say it. "I went to public school, but would that be good enough for your kids? No. So now I'm supposed to walk around with all these important people. And they're all judging me." He stopped for a second. I didn't know why.

My mother opened her mouth to talk, figuring, probably, that he wanted her to say something.

"Don't you dare try to deny that," he said. "Between those two goddamn schools, we've got probably every doctor and lawyer in this city who's got kids. And now they're all going to walk around saying I hate my kid."

"You hate me?" I asked. I'd suspected that for a long time, but I'd never heard him come right out and say it.

"Shut up," he said. "No, I don't hate you. You shouldn't even be listening to this. Get out of here." I didn't move. "I'm just saying that that doctor who called up here is probably running around telling everybody that I must hate my kid if I won't coach basketball."

"Dr. Klinger's really busy," I said. I thought that might make him feel better.

My father pushed past my mother, his hands wide open, ready to grab me around my throat. "I told you to get the hell out of here!" he said.

My mother was trying to push herself in between us. My father got a hold on me, but not a good enough hold to tighten his grasp on my throat where he could cut off my breathing. He was shaking me. My mother pushed back at him. She was such a little woman, probably only five feet tall. My father may have looked like a man with no strength, but he was hefty with all that fat and anger. My mother fell back and hit her head against the side of the counter. It wasn't the corner, and her hair in back cushioned her, but she hit hard. I'd had that kind of hit. It gave you an instant headache. She let out a howl without meaning to. I wanted to tell her not to cry. The last time my father beat her up, it was because she was crying. At least I think it was. She was crying, and he beat her up.

My father let go of me. I was hoping he would reach over and help my mother up. That's sort of what he did, only what he did was grab her arm and jerk her up to her feet so fast that I bet she could have gotten some kind of brain damage. I'd seen it on TV, where a kid would get hit on the football field, and his brain would slam into the back of his head, and then it would get hit from the other side and slam into the front of his head, and at the end of the program he'd be in a wheelchair, all drooling. I was glad St. Michael's had only basketball and soccer. I thought my father should have been, too.

Anyway, he forgot about me. He smacked my mother across the face. I hollered for him to stop. He hollered for me to get my stupid ass out of the room. I saw Ada peek around the door. There was absolutely no expression on her face. She once told me that she'd quit having feelings about our family a long time ago. Both of us knew that wasn't true, but she needed to believe it so she could make it through high school. Besides, she had Finn. Ada caught my eye. With her head she signaled me to get out of the room. With my head I signaled her to get in the room. I thought maybe she could surprise our father into stopping. Three against one. She shook her head, *no*. I shook my head, *yes*. It was just seconds. My father was screaming at my mother. Her hands were in front of her face, and he was swatting them away, grabbing her hair, pulling her head back with one hand so he could hit her with the other. Finally, an expression came over Ada's face that said she knew how this could end. She burst into the room.

"If you don't stop right now, I'll go get your gun," she said.

My father stopped. He looked at Ada. Like he was tempted to go after her next. Then something came over him. Like sadness. But he didn't know we might see it. He was quiet for a moment. "I'm going out," he said. His voice was quiet. "Don't try to call me. I'll be back when I feel better."

CHAPTER THREE

I didn't want to go to school the next morning. Neither did Ada. Both of us had stayed up until three o'clock in the morning, sitting on our mother's bed. Well, maybe I dozed off a few times, but that's worse than staying awake. None of us said anything, but we were thinking that if we stayed together, maybe he wouldn't kill us. My father was the kind of man who said, *I'm going to kill you,* for the smallest reason, like if I spilled a glass of Coke on the table. My mother would ask him not to talk that way, but he said it was just an expression, and we knew Grandmama Fisher said it all the time, too, and so far she hadn't killed anybody. But my father seemed more like a killer than Grandmama. Sometimes he kept his gun in the car. I was riding with him on Carrollton Avenue once and some kids who were maybe my age came off the curb at an intersection with squeegees to clean the windshield. My father hollered at them to stop, and of course they didn't, and he actually reached into the glove compartment and got his gun and jumped out of the car and waved it at them. When he got back in, I was ducked down under the dashboard, and he pulled me up by my shoulder. Mostly so I'd be out of his way when he put the gun back. When I looked out those kids were gone, to say the least.

"Is it loaded?" I'd whispered.

"You'd better believe it's loaded," he said. "Don't ever point a gun unless it's loaded."

My father came home at three o'clock in the morning. We'd all been jumping at every little sound, like the ice maker, for so long that we almost didn't notice.

"What are you two doing up?" he asked when he walked into the bedroom. His voice was soft and friendly. He wasn't drunk. He wasn't a drinker.

Ada didn't say anything. I surely wasn't going to open my mouth. He seemed nice, but I wasn't going to do anything to change that.

"I think it's time for bed, kids," my mother said. He wasn't scary, and she could tell.

"Do we have to go to school?" I said. As soon as the words were out of my mouth I realized that I was sounding like the rotten student that my father didn't like, and I wanted to take them back. But he said, "I'm sure you're tired, so if you have trouble concentrating, you can probably go to the office."

I still didn't think going to school was a good idea.

Being at school was a terrible idea for sure. When you've had almost no sleep, anything can make you feel like crying. Practically the first thing in the morning, I found out what Dr. Klinger had done, and it made me mostly sad. He'd told Ren that my father had said I couldn't play basketball because I needed to come home and do my homework and get my grades up. He said it was no different from being in college. Boys at Tulane had to keep up their grades, or they could get kicked off the team.

"I don't know why your dad won't let you play, and then he could pull you off if your grades drop," Ren said.

"Yeah," I said. Ren's dad had been making him see a psychiatrist ever since he was three. Just to talk about his feelings. Ren once told me that his mother was having a hard time getting pregnant, and if she hadn't gotten pregnant with Ren right when she did, they'd have gone to the Jewish agency to adopt. The thought that I'd almost been Ren was too much for me to think about sometimes. Of course, I wouldn't have been Ren. I'd probably have made even Dr. Klinger mad.

Coach Jorge had taken me aside in P.E. and told me the same story Ren had. By then it was almost lunch time, and I was so sleepy I couldn't think. It was like my vision was closing in on me, and when it reached the middle I was going to fall right down where I was. Coach said, "So if anybody asks, you tell them you'll play when you get good grades." I could feel myself starting to cry, and I hated to cry in front of other kids. Coach pulled me into his office.

"Everybody knows I'll never make good grades," I said. Then I started really crying. I'd completely forgotten that this was a story Dr. Klinger had made up to protect me.

"Hold up, man," Coach said. "Try to stop before guys can see it on your face."

I made myself stop. I figured that after P.E., I'd go to the office and ask to go home.

But when I went to the office, Mrs. Banks just whipped out that Adderall before I could say a word, and I thought maybe I could make it through the afternoon with Adderall, which calmed me down, but really kept people awake no matter who they were, and I didn't want to stress my mother out extra, assuming she was still alive and not murdered, and then I thought about how scared I was, and I drank a lot of water to get that pill into my system fast.

When I got dropped off, both my parents' cars were there. I walked in the front door, and it was completely silent in the house. So the name I called out was, "Ada." No answer. I tiptoed slowly. I watched a lot of reality TV. I knew what was next. I figured I'd better get it over with. I went straight for my mother's studio. She had a counter in the middle under the skylight where she painted her ceramics. Probably I'd see her dead feet sticking out from behind there. Maybe a pool of blood.

There she was, sitting on a stool behind the counter, painting a bowl.

"Oh, wow," I said.

I surprised my mother. She jumped a little. "Otto!" she said. "What's going on?"

"Nothing." That was the question *I* was supposed to ask. "Are you okay?"

She put the bowl down. I actually recognized it. She was painting it yesterday, completely different colors. My mother was kind of famous among the arts people. Even though she wasn't friends with any of them, because my father said they were stupid, and she had a hard time getting together with anybody. She showed her stuff at RHINO Gallery and at the arts fairs and everything. My father thought they were crap. Ada thought they were gorgeous. My mother put them out on shelves in the living room. My father took them down and put books up instead. My mother sold the ones he took down. She could get $300 for a little vase.

"You were worried about me," she said.

I nodded. "I didn't like being at school."

"Well, I think things are going to calm down. Let's go talk to your daddy."

She never called him my daddy. That was not a good sign. He was in the bedroom, and when we walked in, the whole place was a mess. He was packing.

I didn't say a word. I folded my arms across my chest and waited. My father was taking shirts on hangers and holding them up in front of himself, like he was trying to decide whether to take them out on hangers or fold them up. He shrugged, threw them on the bed, and the ones on top started to slide toward the floor. He caught them, threw them back on top. He shrugged again.

"So," he said.

"I don't want you to move out," I said. I surprised myself saying that. I didn't know where it came from.

"I love you, too, son," he said, "but I told your mother that all of you make me too angry, and you kind of force me to hurt you. I think it'd be better if I lived somewhere else."

I looked at my mother out of the corner of my eye. I was hoping that wasn't true. That we all weren't so bad. Being hit was a terrible punishment, but leaving us was even worse. She had no particular expression on her face. She wasn't giving me any signals.

"I can behave better," I said.

He sounded so nice. "I know you think you try," he said. "But you've had so many chances. And we've got you medicated. You're in the best school there is. You just don't take anything seriously. I'm sorry, but enough is enough."

That meant it was all my fault. "What about Ada?" I asked. "What about Mom? You're leaving them because of me?"

I could feel my mother moving around a little bit, even though I wasn't looking at her. I hoped I was standing up for her and maybe making a difference.

"If you recall," my father said, "it was your mother with whom I had the differences last night. I don't think you need to be in the middle of our marital difficulties, okay? We're just going to get a separation, okay? Just a separation."

He was sounding so kind that I wanted him to stay and be my good father. But probably half of the fathers at St. Michael's were divorced dads, and they were good, from what I could see. I slept over at a lot of dad houses, and they actually were a lot of fun. My friends' rooms were messy, and they didn't have too many rules about bedtime, and we ate drive-through a lot.

I asked him if he was going to get joint custody. I knew all the words.

The old version of my father popped out for a second. "Look, right now I'm living in my office. And the rental I've got a bead on has one bedroom. It's not as if I'm rich like all your private school friends."

"Oh," I said, and I walked out of the room. This was my fault. I'd fix it. He'd move back in.

Ada was torn. Half of her was happy to see him gone, and half of her was miserable because he took the gun and the key with him. "We have got to change the locks on the house," she said over dinner the very night he moved out.

"He's not really moved out," my mother said. That was exactly what I was thinking, but maybe not the same way she was. He'd put almost all his winter clothes into his car, plus everything in the bathroom that he always used, which included the towel and washcloth he had hanging in there right then. Then he went to the bookcase where he kept autographed books and pulled about five armloads out. I think about the only thing he said during his packing was when he was loading those books that nobody read after he bought them. "These should be going out in boxes," he said.

"I'm not selling your signed books," my mother said.

He gave her a look that said, *I'm looking down on you because you're poor now and I don't trust you,* and he kept on walking with those terrible fat books.

Anyway, my mother told Ada, "This is just a trial separation. Locking him out isn't going to fix anything."

"Yes, it is," Ada said. "It's going to fix me. What if he decides one night it's time to come in here and kill all of us?"

My mother looked at me to see if I was buying what Ada was saying. I tried to look very scared. I sure had been very scared last night when I thought he definitely was going to come back with his gun. And that afternoon I'd come in looking for my mother's dead body. But up until the last second, my father had seemed like he was very sorry and sad. And even at the last second, he was just sort of like a normal dad who was a little annoyed because his kid was asking for too much, too soon in a hard situation. It was hard to be scared of somebody like that. I thought maybe my father had changed, now that he was doing something this drastic. He'd be back soon.

"I don't think Otto's scared right now," my mother said. She looked at me. "Right?"

I shrugged my shoulders. This was a miserable situation. My mind said I should be scared, but I wasn't. "We were all scared shitless last night," I said. I caught myself. I'd said *shitless*. If I'd said that with my father in the house, I'd already have been a giant flesh blob on the wall. I looked from my mother to Ada and back, and we all burst out laughing.

"Wow, that felt good," Ada said.

"Mmm, hmm," my mother said. "I've got to admit."

In a way, I had to admit it felt like we were on vacation at my house. It was like the times when my father went to something called MLA, which was a convention, and he would be away for three or four days. All of us at home could relax, sort of the way kids could take it easy if a teacher left the room to go to the office or the bathroom or something. We'd behave because we had it in us to behave, but we felt free. That was it. We were free to behave. My mother even said that I was easy to get along with, and what was wrong with me. I had a feeling that having my father out of the house was good for me, but I kind of missed him. Not the actual him, but the fact of him. Or the person of him. Or something. It was confusing.

I knew there was a support group at St. Michael's for kids whose parents were divorced. Like I said before, schools like St. Michael's are loaded with kids that come from broken homes, though you can't tell a kid with divorced parents just by looking at him. I mean, those kids aren't depressed or dressed badly or mean or bullied or anything. They fit right in. I'd been at St. Michael's for eight and a half years, and that meant that a lot of kids in my grade had gone through their parents' divorces, because, let's face it, parents are under the worst stress when they have kids in elementary school. At least that's the way it seemed to me in my house. We weren't cute babies, and we couldn't drive and get around by ourselves, and it cost a lot to send us to school and get us braces and tutors and shrinks and stuff, so naturally parents would get sick of their lives and split up. I'd never paid attention to other kids in my class when their parents divorced. My friends, for some reason, all had parents who were still together. I didn't know much about broken-up homes. I thought maybe I needed the support group. Mrs. Phipps worked with it. I stayed in her room at lunch one day.

"My father moved out," I said.

"Oh, my," she said.

"It was, like, the day after the Thanksgiving play." That was important for her to know. But she just looked at me. "I'm thinking maybe I could be in the support group."

Mrs. Phipps was, like I said, a teacher who'd seen everything. So she was putting me in her mental computer to see what popped out. It took a few seconds, and then she said, "That means your parents have been separated for two weeks?"

I nodded. Two weeks didn't sound like very long. But it had been an awful two weeks. My mother had been running around like crazy finding ways to make a lot of money with her art, like this might be permanent, which meant she was on the phone all the time. Ada said that was her way of not thinking about reality. I wasn't sure what that meant, but as far as I was concerned, I didn't have a mother who could answer any questions. I heard her tell someone on the phone that my father wasn't willing to go to a shrink, but that did me no good. Ada wasn't around much, but then, she never was. I didn't tell my friends because it was too embarrassing. So for days I'd just been inside my own head. And even with Adderall, the inside of my own head was full of stuff that didn't make sense. The only person I thought could help me understand was my father, and I didn't have the nerve to call him. His office number was posted inside the kitchen cabinet door, but I'd never used it before. I wanted to tell him I was sorry.

"Tell you what," Mrs. Phipps finally said. "It's almost Christmas break. This is a really bad time to start anything. The kids in the group are thinking mostly about having a party. Making plans for the holidays. Why don't you do the best you can over Christmas, and after the first of the year, you come to me, and if nothing's changed, we'll introduce you to the group."

"What would change?" I said.

"A lot could change," she said. "And all for the better."

Mrs. Phipps was smiling. Teachers at St. Michael's had to be very positive. Even though usually there was no reason for being that way. At least for kids like me.

My mother grew up with the name Elise Diamond in New Orleans. She had Shebsel Silber on her mother's side and some other Jews on her father's side, but her parents didn't practice being Jews, and she got to have Christmas like all her Protestant and Catholic friends. So I was growing up having Christmas, complete with a tree and presents—and of course Santa Claus, right up until one of Ada's rotten friends told me the truth when I was five.

Even without my father and the money he thought was so important, we got a ten-foot tree. That was a good thing about living in New Orleans. You could live in a house that was a hundred and fifty years old with fourteen-foot ceilings, and even a tall Christmas tree wouldn't hit the ceiling. I was big enough that year to set it up all by myself. The truth was that, even though my father packed a good punch, he didn't have the kind of athletic body a person needs to get a tree set up straight in its stand. We even went out and bought all white lights. My father always insisted on multi-colored lights because Grandmama Fisher liked them. Ada thought they were tacky.

My father was coming over for early Christmas, and I was going to spend the night at his apartment. This had all been worked out at my parents' counselor's office. My father had agreed to go when my mother said it wasn't going to be about blaming anybody, and besides, she'd pay for it. Ada didn't want them to go to counseling. Ada wanted them to see lawyers right away. My mother had told her that maybe they'd get divorced, sounding like she was saying, *Otto, maybe you'll get a new $200 skateboard,* but either way she needed to figure out some stuff. Ada had said, "Okay, I can see that," sounding like she knew everything, and I sort of had a feeling she did. Anyway, the counselor said my father should come over to the house before Christmas to be part of the family. Ada said, "Okay, he can see how great we're doing without him, but I won't be here."

My mother said, "Listen, we make him so angry. Please be here. We have to stop making him so mad."

I'd looked at Ada. It was a very important moment. "What the hell are you talking about?" she asked. We hadn't graduated to the F word yet. "We make *him* angry?"

My mother said, "I'm the adult here. I don't think I should have to talk about adult matters with the two of you."

Ada folded her arms across her chest. "I'm going to be eighteen in March. I can vote in the next election. I can join the Army. Shit, I *ought* to join the Army. Go around Tulane telling everybody that genius David Fisher's kid's a private in the U.S. Army."

I was thinking to myself that the military might be where I was going to wind up, but I didn't say anything. My father had threatened me with it more than once. Of course, he always threw in that an IED would blow off both of my legs and leave me so bad off, with no way to get around and no education, that I'd be homeless.

Anyway, my mother sighed the way she always sighed when Ada won an argument. It wasn't a sad sigh, more of a proud sigh. "I guess there's no point sending Otto out of the room," my mother said. "The counselor says I push your father's buttons. That's why he hits me."

"What?" I said. I was only thirteen, but even I knew that was wrong. There's never a reason to hit anybody. You didn't have to go to college anymore to learn about how people act with each other. You could just go to kindergarten. Or watch Dr. Phil and Oprah and Anderson Cooper. I never would have chosen to watch those programs if I'd had my own TV, but sometimes my mother left on those shows, and there was nothing else on. She'd be in the kitchen, obviously not paying attention, and I'd hear bits and pieces. I'd do a math problem, listen to some girl holler at her mother with Anderson Cooper in the middle, and I'd get the general idea of who was wrong and who was right. You could tell just looking at Anderson Cooper. He was a cool guy and probably would have made a cool dad, but he was gay. He still could have been a dad, but he wasn't.

"The counselor says that when I go too far and don't let up, your father feels like I'm cornering him, and all he can do is lash out with his fists," my mother said to me. "It's the way men react. Fight or flight. Sometimes he leaves, you know that."

Ada walked over to my mother and put her hands on her shoulders. She was gentle, because putting her hands on her shoulders could look bad if she did it wrong. "Mama, that counselor needs to be fired."

"She's been in practice for almost forty years." My mother suddenly looked like she was the youngest, most innocent person in the room. Ada put her arms around her and hugged, but my mother left her arms at her sides. Not because she didn't want to hug back, it seemed to me, but because she didn't know what to do about anything.

"I love you, Mama," Ada said, "but I'm not going to be here when he comes."

We'd had visitors to our house before, but no one ever was as friendly and courteous and full of compliments as my father. "I don't remember this place being as warm and attractive as it is," he said as he walked into the living room. He even told my mother that the vases and bowls that she'd placed on the shelves where his books had been looked very "aesthetically pleasing," which made my mother turn pink. She ate it all up, like she was winning something. "I have to admit, a tree with white lights gives the room a wonderful ambience," he said. He ate most of the plate of cookies my mother had bought at Whole Foods, which was too bad, because those cookies cost $14.95 for eight, and they were really good. He drank two cups of eggnog, with no whiskey in them. I was trying to remember everything so I could tell

Ada. She could pretend she didn't care, but she'd want to know. I thought she'd especially want to know how much he ate. First of all, she'd enjoy being disgusted at how greedy he was. But more important, she'd be able to think about how he'd get fatter and get diabetes and die all afraid, with just Grandmama Fisher sitting next to him, telling him he couldn't have any morphine. That was a fantasy she always talked about. Not the fatness and diabetes, but the deathbed.

We all sat on the edges of our seats, and it was like watching two kids in my class on a date. They didn't have anything to say to each other. So they talked through me. "Otto's sleeping over," my father said.

"Yes, he's looking forward to it. Aren't you?" My mother looked at me.

I nodded. I was working a cookie for all I was worth, hoping I'd get a second one. My father was putting them away at an alarming speed.

"I see he's all packed up," my father said. "You packed up all your homework?"

I figured I'd better say something. "I've got a lot tonight," I said.

"He didn't get a chance to do it yet," my mother said. "He was helping me get the house ready for your visit."

My father started to say something but stopped himself. I could see it happen. He looked around. "Great job," he said.

"I put up the tree all by myself," I said. I hoped that was all right to say.

"You're a lot better than I am at it."

Shit, where was this going? Was my mother going to give their counselor a report card? Was I supposed to tell Ada my father was a whole new person? Whatever was going on, I liked it. If he could keep acting like this, life sure would be better. He would come home and love me.

"Thanks," I said.

CHAPTER FOUR

It lasted as long as he could stand it. Maybe the counselor had been right. His buttons got pushed. My Adderall had to wear off so I could sleep at night, so he quit being able to stand me. When I say the Adderall wore off, I think I mean that no matter how hard I tried, I quit acting like an adult and started back acting like I was thirteen, but with my father you had to be an adult. Though Ada was almost legally an adult, and my mother had been an adult for a long time, so there was no way of knowing until my father spent a few hours with each of them. Which wasn't happening any time soon.

I was a little excited on the way over to his place. It was like getting a tour of a famous person's house, which I'd actually never done before. I mean, I'd been dragged along by my parents and school to look at plantations around New Orleans and old houses in Washington, D.C. and Massachusetts and even Lincoln's cabin. And for part of those times I'd liked trying to pretend living in those places, which would have been horrible because absolutely none of them had bathrooms. Also, even though they had air conditioning or heat now, the tour guides always got a kick out of saying, "Imagine what it was like with no air conditioning," or "Imagine having to rely on chopping wood to keep warm." Anyway, visiting my father was going to be the same, only different. I figured he'd have a bathroom and heat, but I wondered what he was doing for a bed and other stuff. I might learn something about him. Such as whether he could take care of himself.

He was renting half of a little double-shotgun house. It was kind of cute, and probably very cheap because it was on the bad side of St. Charles Avenue.

"This is it," he said, walking in ahead of me, not looking back at me, maybe not wanting to know how I reacted.

The place had a lot of furniture. Really ugly furniture, old lady furniture. Too old for my Oma Diamond, who was a pretty cool lady and had gorgeous antiques. This was dusty cheap stuff with dark wood all cut into flower designs and dark green velvety seats and armrests. Kind of like somebody a hundred years ago was trying to copy the Queen of England or something.

There was one bedroom with a double bed. The same dark wood. I hoped I wasn't going to sleep in there with him. He saw me following him, and I'm sure he expected me to wonder where I was sleeping because he'd had to think about it, too. "I bought you some sheets," he said. "The sofa in the living room is actually pretty comfortable. I've tried it out for you."

"It's kind of scary in the front," I said. "I mean, if somebody breaks in, they'll get me first." This was a crummy neighborhood. I knew it, and he knew it.

"You want them to get me first?" he asked, and he meant it.

I shrugged, which to me meant, *Actually, yes.*

"Look, there's nothing to worry about. First of all, any criminal with any sense, and by that I mean criminal sense, is not breaking in at the street door. He's going to try the back. And even if he's all hopped up on crack and tries the front, there's a deadbolt, so he's going to probably fail, and while he's failing, he's going to make so much noise you'll be all the way to the kitchen before anything happens. You can turn on my light as you pass me."

I didn't think I was going to get a lot of sleep.

When we got to the kitchen, I automatically opened the refrigerator. "Hey, a little politeness there," my father said.

"I'm a visitor?" I asked. I was hoping by then that he was going to want some kind of custody. I wasn't sure I wanted it in real life, but I definitely wanted to have it to talk about when we went back to school and I joined the support group. Besides, his wanting it would be nice. I'd already had two parents give me away. I'd never thought about that before, but I'd heard somebody say that on Dr. Phil, and it made a lot of sense.

"I guess you're not technically a visitor," my father said.

There was almost nothing in the refrigerator. Whole milk, pineapple juice, a loaf of white bread, and butter. None of that had ever been in the refrigerator at home.

"You trying to figure something out?" he said while I stood at the open door of the refrigerator.

I probably was, but I didn't know what. "I don't know," I said.

He told me we'd send out for pizza, and I could have Sprite. There he was, with nothing for good health in his house except maybe juice, and he was going to dictate what I could eat. He knew that caffeine affected me. He didn't know the sugar in Sprite was probably just as bad. "I could just have some pineapple juice," I said.

"Hell, no," he said. "Do you know how much trouble it is to lug that crap home from the grocery?"

I didn't say anything. He probably literally weighed twice as much as my mother, and she went to the grocery twice a week and carried in a couple of gallons of stuff for him to drink.

Homework got started too late to have any success. I was full of sugar and pizza additives and empty of Adderall, and my brain was jumping, and today was the very first day we had talked about the Distributive Law in math class, and I felt no hope. Usually, I'd ask Ada to talk me through it. Or if Ada wasn't home, I'd ask my mother. She could take the textbook and read the lesson, then teach it to me. It would all come back to her from seventh grade, *easy-peasy,* she said. My mother was an artist, but she said she could go back and forth between right brain and left brain, as long as she wasn't asked to be on both sides at the same time.

My father was in the front room, and I was at the formica table in the kitchen, and after I'd read the lesson over at least a dozen times without making sense, I knew I had to ask him for help.

"Do you know anything about the Distributive

Law?" I asked when I walked into the front room. He was reading a student paper, using a little lap desk. He'd made it clear that he was making a sacrifice of the table so I could do my homework.

"Hold on, there," he said. "I can't just stop in the middle here." He held one finger up in the air, like I was interrupting an important phone conversation or something. A good minute must have passed, and I was getting impatient. I looked at my book again, hoping it would make sense. I must have sighed, because he slapped the paper down and asked, "So what is so extremely urgent?"

I told him I was sorry, but we were learning the Distributive Law, and if I didn't use it, I couldn't do my assignment.

I saw his eyes dart to my book. He had no idea what subject this law had to do with. For all he knew, it was social studies or science. All he knew for sure was that it wasn't English. "Look," he said, "I'm an English professor. When you specialize in using your verbal skills, you let your math skills atrophy." He paused. "Atrophy means to wither up."

"Mom's an artist, but she can do math," I said. I was about to suggest that he probably could, too, but he interrupted me.

"I'm sure your mother is superior to me in many ways," he said. He was getting angry.

"That's not what I meant." I hoped I sounded apologetic.

He told me to hand over the book. I pointed out the half of the page where it explained the law. I had a blank sheet of paper. "Look," I said. I drew a rectangle, divided not in equal parts. I labeled one b and one c. I labeled the side a. "So I'm supposed to know that a (b+c) = ab + ac. That's what Mrs. Phipps told us."

"So what?" my father said "Sounds like you get it."

I told him to look at the problems. They said things like "5 (7 + 3) =" and "2 (x + 4) =."

"This is a royal pain in the neck," he said. "I thought you were just coming over here for a quiet evening. You never cause this kind of trouble at home. Other kinds, but not this."

He said "home."

"What?" I asked.

"Have you heard one word I said?" I didn't want to tell him what word I heard, so I nodded. "I don't think so," he said. ""You need to pay attention. Maybe you don't pay attention to anybody else, but you need to pay attention to me."

"Okay."

He must have read over that half-page explanation of the Distributive Law four times, but it clearly made no sense to him. Here was a man who thought he could read poems that made no sense to anybody, but when it came to math, he was no better than me.

He slammed the book shut. "What did your goddamn teacher tell you about this?" he asked. "You just have to teach it back to me, and then you'll have it."

"Mrs. Phipps is not goddamn."

"If she didn't make you understand this crap, then she deserves to be teaching in a school like that."

I was kind of used to getting my feelings hurt, but he was being mean about a very sweet lady, and he was being mean by saying that my school sucked. "You don't know Mrs. Phipps," I said. "She's really nice."

"Really nice doesn't cut it, son. Do you think if I were really nice that my students would learn one thing about how poorly they write, not to mention how poorly they read?"

I shrugged.

All of a sudden, he picked up my math book and slammed it down onto the floor. It made a good loud noise which kind of surprised me. "Jesus Christ," he said. "I swear sometimes your ADHD is contagious. Look what you've done. You've come in here to do your homework, which looks like it's just a step above five plus five, and I'm here defending myself as a teacher!"

"It's not five plus five," I said. "It's algebra."

He tried to get up and get me and the lap desk out of his space. But he was so heavy on the bottom that he couldn't do it without hands, and I had to admit he looked pretty funny, kind of grunting and thinking I couldn't see him, a fat, angry man, stuck on that ugly sofa, trying to push off with his big old legs with his arms out in front of him holding that lap desk. He didn't think I knew what he was trying to do, but he was getting redder and redder in the face. Finally, he threw the lap desk down on top of my book, and he used his hands to push himself up off the sofa, and he was up, standing over me.

That was the standoff of all my nightmares. Him over me. I was tall enough to look him in the eye now, but when he was over me, it was like I was five or six, and he was powerful, and he was going to smack my face with his open hand, then beat me with his closed fist, and I was just a skinny little boy. I stood up fast. But it made no difference. He was too angry. In the seconds it took for me to stand up and get my balance, he grabbed me by the shoulders and slammed me against the wall. I almost lost my footing, but I didn't. My head hit the wall. Hard. Harder than my mother's head had hit the counter a few weeks ago. I didn't have any hair to protect me. All I could think was, *Am I passing out? I need to know, because if I get a concussion, nobody's going to do anything except me.*

I didn't pass out. I went from the split second of hitting the wall to meeting my father's eyes six inches from my own. I could smell his breath. My friends told me that if you ate the same thing as a girl, you wouldn't smell each other's breath, but that wasn't true. He stank of rotten pizza. I didn't think I did. He had me pinned, and he slammed me again. But this time I held my head forward, so only my back hit the wall. "It's not five plus five, it's algebra," he said in a girly voice. Then he slammed me again. "If you're doing algebra in seventh grade when I didn't get algebra until tenth grade, you must be some kind of genius I don't know about. I *definitely* don't know about."

I forgot for just that second about wanting him to come home. I forgot about trying to be an adult. We were in a double-shotgun, and I'd seen the neighbor lady when she came home. If he shot me, he'd go to prison. "You saw the xs," I said loud, not caring. "That's algebra."

"Do you ever want to come over here again?" he asked. This time he was practically screaming.

"I'm the one who wanted to see you," I said. "You don't see Ada trying, do you?"

At that he punched me in the stomach, and I let out

an animal kind of sound in spite of myself. It was kind of like how a dog screams when you step on its foot.

That's when we heard a knocking on the wall my father shared with the lady who lived in the other side of the shotgun.

"You need to be quiet," he said, his voice low. "She owns this place. All I need is to get thrown out. I'm a professor at Tulane."

"Well, don't hit me," I said. It seemed to me that people with PhDs probably didn't hit other people. I didn't know why I thought that, but I kind of associated educated people with acting civilized. It was probably that Grandmama Fisher hadn't finished high school, and she definitely was the hitting type. People like Grandmama Fisher were always on shows like *Jerry Springer* and *Maury Povich*.

He didn't unpin me. I was still up against the landlady's wall. I could have bet the lady was leaning against the wall right then with her ear as wide open as she could get it. I was going to make sure she heard everything. "Why won't you let me go?" I asked. "I can just call my friend Ren and get him to help me. Or I'll call Mom."

"You're just trying to push all my buttons, huh? Why don't you just call up Ren's father and say, 'Oh, Dr. Klinger, I'm sure you can do everything a good father can do, so would you please help me with my arithmetic homework?'"

"Please don't say that. I said I was sorry about basketball."

"You are such a piece of crap," he said, and I knew he was loud enough to be heard through the wall, so I pretended to start sobbing loudly. I was confused. He needed to come home. But he needed to behave first.

Sure enough, a knock came at the door in a matter of seconds.

We were about twelve feet from the door, so my father whispered, but I could hear that he meant business. "I swear, if you get me thrown out of this place, you will never hear the end of it. You hear me?"

I nodded. I knew getting thrown out wouldn't mean moving back home.

I backed away from him. I was sure he was hoping that I'd back all the way out of the room so he could make the lady think she'd been hearing the radio or something. She was a lot older than he was, and she was black, and I knew my father figured he could outsmart her on anything. He had even less use for black people than he did for Jews. He might have learned more about literature than Grandmama Fisher, but he hadn't learned more about liking different people.

"Good evening, Mrs. Morris," he said. He probably wasn't fooling her with his politeness because he wasn't fooling me at all.

Mrs. Morris was cool. "You all having some difficulties over here?" she said. As nice as you please. I could tell already that she was smarter than my father in all the ways that counted.

"No, ma'am," my father said. He was looking down on her. I could tell. She probably could tell, too.

Mrs. Morris looked past him to me. "You doing okay, son?"

I waited a fraction of a moment before I nodded.

I figured she'd catch on that I was lying, but my father wouldn't be able to call me on it.

"Listen, Dr. Fisher," she said. "This isn't the best neighborhood in the world, and I know you hear noise in the streets, but I've got these properties, and I'm not having them be a source of the trouble, no."

Mrs. Morris had properties. More than one. She had power. My father had a PhD, and he was renting. I hoped Grandmama Fisher would come down to visit. Wait until she heard Mrs. Morris speak better English than she did.

I could tell my father was feeling it. "This is just temporary," he said.

Mrs. Morris looked at me like she was saying she'd been around a long time and knew a lot. "A six months' lease is not what you call temporary," she said. "Matter of fact, I'd say most six month's leases go into at least one more six months' lease." She stopped for a second. "As long as I don't throw a person out."

My father put his hand on the door, meaning he was putting her out. She hollered over his shoulder to me. "You know my name. You need me, you just call my name. Old people don't sleep too well."

As soon as the door was closed, and my father had spun around, I said, "I think I need to go home."

"I don't think so," he said. "That's exactly what people like your mother and that woman want. I'm as good a parent as anybody. You're going to spend the night, and it's going to be fine."

I told him my bedtime was 8:30. He didn't know any different. I lay there in the dark for two hours before I fell asleep, but it was a good idea. I think that before I dozed off I pretty much figured out the Distributive Law. But when I woke up, it was gone.

The next morning was my mother's turn to carpool. It seemed to me that she should have been getting a break for the first time in thirteen years, not needing to get up to do anything for me. But when I'd asked my father if he was going to drive carpool, he'd acted like I was insane. It was one thing to deal with one kid, and a few times he'd been forced to deal with two kids, either me and Ada or me and a friend, but there was no way he was going to voluntarily run around town picking up four strange, smelly kids for no reason. Just for starts, he said, it would be wear and tear on his car. "All of you have giant, filthy sneakers, and I've got leather seats," he said, ending the conversation.

So my mother came to the front of his house to pick me up before she went to get everybody else. I'd been sitting on the stoop since eight o'clock to keep her from having to honk and annoy Mrs. Morris or, worse, to have to get out and ring my father's doorbell. It was freezing out there, but I didn't mind. Every now and then, my father would open the door an inch to be sure no crack fiend had kidnapped me. I told him that didn't happen to white kids in black neighborhoods. That happened to white kids in the country where only white people live. He said I didn't know anything. I could have told him that you can learn a lot from reality TV, but I knew where that would take us.

When I popped into the front seat of my mother's

car, I must have let out a huge sigh, because my mother said, "You're pretty happy to be leaving, huh?" I threw my arms around her neck and hugged her. I didn't need to say anything. She put the car in park.

"I didn't get my homework done," I whispered into her ear. I felt her body laughing. "Not too funny," I said into her ear.

"We'll do it right here," she whispered back into my ear.

She left the heat on, and I told her it was about the Distributive Law, and that my father couldn't understand it any better than I could. I was just giving her information, but she looked kind of pleased. In fact, it was the best I'd seen her look in quite a while. I gave her the book to look at. The cover was a little messed up from where it had hit the floor the night before, but she didn't notice. It only took her about two minutes to read the half-page explanation. "Remember when we did the Associative Law?" I nodded. That had been easy. All it said was that it didn't matter what order you put stuff in on either side of the equals sign. My mother had made a little scale and shown me how it worked. "Okay," she said, "give me a sheet of paper." I gave her a sheet of paper, and sitting right there in front of my father's house, she tore it up into tiny pieces and showed me how the Distributive Law worked. It was so easy, and it was so much relief, that I jumped almost high enough to hit the roof of the car when my father came out and banged on my window.

"What the hell are you doing out here?" he asked.

The window was so fogged up that I only knew it was my father because he was a white guy in the same blue shirt I'd seen him in a few minutes before. I rolled down the window. My mother leaned across me. "You want him to do his homework, so we're doing his homework," she said.

"Not in front of my goddamn house," he said. "People will think you're crazy."

He could probably see us laughing like we *were* crazy when we pulled off burning rubber. I did half of the problems out loud before we picked up the first kid, even though my numbers were written all shaky on the page. When I got to school I felt good, because I knew I could survive staying at my father's house until he moved back home. As long as I had a way to do homework with my mother in the morning. Oh, yeah, and as long as my father didn't kill me. Which I figured Mrs. Morris could come in with a key and stop. She was skinny, and I didn't think black women in New Orleans worked out unless they were under thirty or something, but I knew she could take my father with both hands tied behind her back.

CHAPTER FIVE

This time Mrs. Phipps probably didn't think she was stepping into it, but I knew better. So did everybody else, even Aiden and Emily, who'd been at St. Michael's five months and had pretty much figured everybody out fast enough. It was another chance for good, old Samantha to play the "poor me, I'm adopted" card.

Mrs. Phipps thought it would be interesting for us to do a language arts project on our names. Not our last names, because that would have put Samantha back on the Mayflower with her make-believe Worthingtons or whatever they were. Mrs. Phipps thought we should research our first names, which, she said, used to be called our Christian names before everything got politically correct and people in the country realized that not everybody was Christian. She said she'd like us to explore the meanings of our names and why our parents chose them.

Up shot Samantha's hand. Mrs. Phipps called on her, and I was sure I saw just a little smile on Mrs. Phipps's face. There was no way that being adopted played into this one.

"Well, like, you know I'm adopted, right?" Samantha

said, and Mrs. Phipps nodded with patience. I knew Samantha couldn't wait. "So, see? My mom told me that my birth mother gave me a name on my original birth certificate. Nobody can see it because it's, um, what do you call it? Well, you can't see it because it's a closed adoption, but the worker told her my original name was Carrie. Like I think there was an actress with that name."

Carrie Fisher. *Star Wars.* I knew that one all right. But I was waiting to see if anybody would raise their hand and say that there was also a horror movie about someone named Carrie. Nobody did, and I figured that if my name was Fisher, I had a right. My hand shot up, not at all as neatly as Samantha's. "Hey, her last name's Fisher." Everybody laughed. "But there's also a horror movie called *Carrie.*" Most of the boys laughed again. All except Nate. He was held back in the pre-K he went to before he came to St. Michael's, so he was a little older than everybody, and he was starting to really like girls. Because he wasn't that bright, he liked Samantha.

It's not that I didn't like girls. When I was alone in the bathroom, I liked the idea of girls a lot. I wouldn't have told anybody this, but the actress Emma Watson was the girl I thought about almost every time. She didn't have a hot body or anything, but I thought about her in the movies, and she was my fantasy girl, and I didn't know any girl in real life like that, and I probably never would.

Samantha's arms were folded across her sorry little excuse for a chest. She was getting boobies like all the other girls, but there were boys in my class with boobies just as big. She gave me a dirty look. It was almost like she was saying, *You're jealous because you only got one name ever, and it's a stupid one.*

Mrs. Phipps took a nanosecond look at the wall clock. She was just as interested in lunch as we were. "This feels like it's getting way off track," she said, "but really it isn't. Samantha, if you want to do two research projects, you may, but you'll have a hard time finding out why you were named Carrie."

"Will I get extra credit?" Samantha asked.

"No," Mrs. Phipps said.

Mrs. Phipps was the best. I'd told her that I wasn't going to do the support group. All she'd said was, "Oh?" And all I'd had to say was, "Yep."

I thought researching my name was one assignment I could do at my father's house and that he would be glad to help me. I thought he might even like it enough that he'd let me use his new computer and printer. When he lived at home we'd all had to share, and Ada had decided long ago that it was better to go work in the computer lab at school or at Finn's house than to fight for time at home. When my father left, she put all the equipment in her room, and it stayed there for the one day it took my mother to discover what she'd done. "Oh, well," Ada had said as she reinstalled everything in the family room. "I don't care. If he left me with nothing more than a number two pencil, it'd still be worth it."

"Why's my name Otto?" I asked my father.

We were in his kitchen. He actually was sitting at the table with me, and I was eating my leftover lunch. I'd figured out that if I bought chips and a drink from the vending machines at lunchtime at school, I'd have something to eat when I got to my father's house. He didn't believe in snacking. At least not for kids. He was sitting there cutting slices off a giant salami and stuffing it into his mouth, washing it down with Coke.

"You don't like the name Otto?" he asked, and he wasn't being mean.

He couldn't have blamed me if I didn't like the name Otto. It was a cartoon name, really. But a lot of kids had stupid names. Movie stars were giving their kids really crazy names, so nobody got picked on over names. Especially at St. Michael's, where nobody really got picked on for anything, except maybe liking a girl. "That's not why I'm asking," I said. "We have to do a paper on how we got our names."

My father thought that one over for a while. He was always looking for a reason why St. Michael's was wasting time not teaching great literature. "Not a bad idea," he said. "Lots of literary criticism focuses on the derivation of characters' names in fiction."

I had no clue what he meant, but that was what he wanted. All I heard was "not a bad idea," and that was good enough, and I asked him if he'd work on it with me.

"You mean the way your mother does? Sit next to you and spell out every word? You had your medicine?"

So much for thinking this was going to be fun. I shrugged. "Do you know how aggravating it is when you do that?" he said.

"Sorry," I said. Now I was past wanting to have fun and on to wanting to get my homework done.

That was good enough for him. He put away the

salami, but he didn't wash his hands. He just wiped them on a paper towel, like getting the grease off was going to get rid of that meaty, garlicky smell on his fingers. I wasn't somebody who paid much attention to how stuff smelled, but he really stank. I hoped he wasn't going to put his hands all over my homework, but he left the table and came back with a pad of yellow lined paper. I shifted my peanut-butter sandwich into my left hand and took the pencil he gave me.

"So what do you know about why we named you Otto?" he said.

I knew what Ada had told me. I couldn't remember the word for it, but my father wouldn't expect me to. "You wanted me to match Ada. Her name's the same back and front, so you picked a boy name that's the same back and front. That's what she told me."

"Palindrome."

"Right, palindrome!"

"So what more do you need from me?" my father asked.

I could see me writing a two-sentence essay and turning it in. It would make me look stupid, and it would make my parents look stupider.

"If I write just that, it'll look stupid," I said. "For starts, it'll be too short. Besides, Mrs. Phipps'll say that there are sure to be other names that are, what? Pala... palin... palindromes. And she'll want to know if Ada is named that just because she's a palindrome, which I guess I could tell, but it's off the subject."

"Tell me boy names that are the same back and forth," my father said. "It's not easy."

I had to think. Of course, I went through all the

vowels and couldn't come up with anything. But then as soon as I started with consonants, I hit Bob right away. "Bob," I said.

"Bob's not a real name," my father said. "Look, I'll tell you about Otto, but you better not tell your mother."

So this was what being from a broken home could be like. Keeping secrets. It didn't feel so bad. I'd be important to him. "Sure," I said.

In a secret-telling voice, my father told me how I got the name Otto. And it all sounded very thoughtful. Mostly.

"Your mother and I naturally shared a love of the arts, or we never could have connected," he said. "We met in a twentieth-century literature class, and we were reading Nabokov. Let me tell you, his novel *Ada* was breathtaking."

I didn't blink. I'd seen the book on the shelf. It was almost two inches thick. That was a long time to hold your breath. I couldn't imagine reading that many pages in my lifetime.

"I think we fell in love over that book," he said. "So of course we'd name our first child Ada. Now when we adopted you, we thought it would be fun to give a boy a palindromic name. I remember the best was Pip, because that's literary, which you'd know by now if your school had a decent reading program. But really, Pip Fisher? It sounds like a baseball player."

I wrote the name Pip on the yellow tablet under where I'd written "Nabockoff."

"There are a lot of names that sound Jewish, so we couldn't use them, and then there's Idi, but Idi Amin was evil, and he was black, and everybody knows that."

I asked him how to spell that. It sounded like "eedy" to me, and that wasn't the same back and forth. He took the pencil with his salami hand and wrote "Idi Amin" on the paper. "You probably don't need to include that," he said.

"We were pretty much left with Abba and Otto, and Abba sounded like the musical group, so then we had to think about what Otto meant."

"Sounds like *auto*," I said, and then I caught myself. "I guess it can't mean that, though, because it's an old name, and cars haven't been around forever."

My father looked at me with what kind of looked like disgust. "An auto is an *automobile,* and the *auto* part of that comes from a word meaning *self.* It's Greek. I don't expect them to be teaching you Greek over there, but what the hell *are* they teaching you?"

"I just learned that from this assignment," I said.

"Touché," he said. I grinned, and he even gave me a little smile. "Look," he said, "we didn't look up the meaning of the name Otto. That's sort of like looking up your astrological sign. We just had to sort out what the name connotes to people in society. As I said, we couldn't name you Idi, because people would think of an evil dictator."

A black one, I thought, but things were going well, so I wasn't saying anything.

"So there've been two famous Ottos that I can think of, and here's the truth. Don't put this in your paper, all right?" I nodded very happily. I was going to be my father's friend. I had a feeling this was going to be a new thing for him. "The Otto your mother liked was Otto Preminger. He was a movie director, and she loved this movie called *Bonjour, Tristesse*. It's the kind of movie you'll never want to see."

I tried to imagine what kind of movie I would never want to see. I knew what *bonjour* meant, and it sounded kind of happy, but the fact that it was French was probably the tip-off. I wasn't going to go to any movie in a foreign language. It was probably in black and white.

"*Tristesse* means sadness," my father said. I got the point. "So your mother thinks you're named after Otto Preminger, and that's okay by me. But your Grandmama Fisher thinks you're named after Otto von Bismarck."

I'd never heard of Otto von Bismarck, so I asked my father to explain. He refused. He said he'd spoon-fed me too much of my homework already, and now it was time for me to work on my own. If I needed more information than he'd given me, I could look it up on Google. He'd let me borrow his computer for the evening. I wrote down "Bizmark," and I kept my eyes down. He was not going to see my face.

Giving a kid with ADHD a computer when his Adderall is wearing off is not a good idea. I was on Facebook for half an hour when I heard my father coming to the back to use the bathroom. Shotgun houses are weird. The kitchen is at the back, and the bathroom is behind it. I switched fast to the Word page I'd set up for my essay, and I started typing fast while he was using the toilet. Lucky for me, he was the sort who went in there for a long time. I didn't want to think what he was doing in there, and I was so close to the door that I was worried that I'd hear something. He must have read my mind, because he turned on the water in the sink and left it running the whole time he was in there. In the meantime, I typed right on the screen everything I knew about Ada and palindromes and Idi and Pip, and it filled up more than a half page, double-spaced. It needed to be 500 words. Good thing I still had a lot more to tell about. This was actually going to be interesting. When other people read theirs, I mean. Like Ren, whose parents had obviously never heard of *Ren and Stimpy*, or they'd never have called their kid the same thing as a cartoon cat whose partner called him a "fat bloated idiot." Ren told me he was named after the writer Reynolds Price, and that his parents knew him personally when they went to Duke. Ren told me that in about second grade, and it didn't mean anything to me. It still didn't mean anything to me, but it sounded like it must have been pretty great, and I figured Ren was going to explain it in class. I also wanted to see what Samantha was going to come up with.

My father came out of the bathroom, and the second he opened the door I could tell he hadn't been in there jerking off. I didn't know what grownups did, but it seemed to me that if a guy went into the bathroom for more than three minutes, he'd be jerking off. He left the door wide open, and the kitchen began to smell awful, and I wondered how people a hundred years ago could eat in their kitchens and have the bathroom right there.

"How's it going?" he asked, but he didn't stop for my answer. He didn't even stop to see that I wasn't goofing off on Facebook, and I was sort of sorry I'd bothered to get down to work. "I've got half a page," I called after him.

I went onto Google to look up some of the stuff on my

list. I didn't have a clue how to spell those guys' names, but Google was usually pretty helpful if you gave them a few letters. I started with Preminger. I was saving the best for last. I typed in "p-r-e-m-m..." and got nothing about a movie director. I tried "bonjour t..." and I got T-shirts, and that took me to some good places, but then I made myself go back. I thought I'd try Bismarck. I typed in the way it sounded, "b-i-z...," but that did me no good.

I was about to give up. Either I wouldn't do my assignment, or I'd go to my father and ask him how to spell those names, and let him tell me how rotten St. Michael's was. Then I realized I'd been on Facebook, and it was my secret way out of his house without him knowing. The person I'd message was Ada. She wasn't working that night. Maybe she was home. Or maybe she was at Finn's and working on his computer. They were enough in love, she once told me, that they didn't have to prove it all the time.

She was online to chat, so I asked her how to spell Preminger and Bismarck. "Those are Ottos," she wrote back. "What are you doing?" I told her I was writing a paper on where I got my name. "Mom says you're named after Otto Preminger. And you're a palindrome like me, of course."

I told her, okay, so that's how you spell Preminger. But what about Bismarck?

"What do you mean, what about Bismarck? Otto von Bismarck was the guy who laid the foundation for Hitler's Third Reich. Hitler named his biggest battleship after him. That's a terrible Otto. We studied him in European history."

I just sat there, staring at the screen.

"You there?" Ada wrote.

"Holy shit," I wrote back.

"So why do you need to know about Bismarck?" Ada wrote.

"Because Dad says Grandmama Fisher thinks I'm named after him."

This time it was Ada's turn not to answer for a while. I wondered what she was doing. When she came back, I could see she was typing furiously. "I was so tempted to tell Mom, but there's no reason to hurt her feelings more than they're already hurt. That man is such a piece of shit. And Grandmama's a bigger piece of shit. She could send me all those cheap, stupid presents, but she's nothing but a racist pig. I swear, your father married Mom just to punish his mother. Did you know he wrote her and said he was marrying a girl named Elise Diamond, and Grandmama wrote back and said, 'I don't know nothing about this girl, if she's a Jew or a Negro or what.' Your father told that story a lot, like he was proud of it or something."

Your father. She'd already quit claiming him as hers.

All I wanted right then was to be with Ada. I didn't know what to say. I sure didn't want to be in the house with my father, who probably always hated my mother. But he was my only father. "I don't know what to do," I wrote back. "I need to be with you."

"Listen, sweet baby Otto," she wrote, "you still think you need your daddy. I love you, but we've got a little problem."

I told her I was really upset. I didn't want to be at my dad's right then. She asked if I wanted her and Finn to come get me. I thought about it. "No," I wrote finally. "He'll know he got to me with the Bismarck stuff. I'm not going to let him get to me."

Ada spelled everything I needed her to spell. I stayed off Facebook. And I concentrated like my life depended on it. I wrote almost 700 words. And I told about how my mother thought I was named after Otto Preminger, but my father secretly had told his mother I was named after Otto von Bismarck. Then I told how my Grandmama Fisher lived in South Carolina and didn't know much about world history, so I couldn't blame her for not understanding people like my mother and Shebsel Silber.

When I finished, I put the paper into my social studies folder. It felt right, and by right, I mean it felt right for me. I didn't need my father or mother to see it. I'd sent it as an attachment to Ada, but only because I needed to protect it in case it fell into the wrong hands. I also felt like I had a little something to prove to her. I brought my father his laptop back. I thought maybe he'd let me play on it or watch TV as a reward for finishing.

He wouldn't take my word that I was finished. I pulled out the three sheets of paper and held them up. I was far enough away that he could see I really had done the assignment, and not close enough for him to make out any of the words.

"I was not born yesterday," he said, and he made this come-here-give-it-to-me motion with his hand.

"Hey, it's kind of private," I said.

"I'm not going to mark up your mistakes," he said. "You're not going to have to do it over."

I suggested that it was kind of long, that maybe he

didn't want to waste his time. That just set him up to remind me that he read college students' papers ten times that long every day, all day, and they were a lot more sophisticated than I would ever be. This was coming from a man who always was talking about how stupid Tulane students were.

I handed it over. I thought about leaving the room. At least I'd had the good sense to send it to Ada. He could tear it up, and I still could retrieve that e-mail in the computer lab at school tomorrow.

I knew where Grandmama was on the page. I could see him get to that part. He kind of hated his mother, but he couldn't stand for anybody else to hate her. "You've got a lot of nerve," he said, his face all red, not looking up. "This woman did not want to accept anyone who was not her own flesh and blood, but she made you feel just like her own grandchild, and this is what you tell people about her? That she's an ignorant hick?"

"That's what you say about her." I said it all matter-of-fact. I figured my only chance was to be his friend, to act like he and I felt the same way about Grandmama.

He didn't say a word. He slapped me across the face so hard I could feel the metal of his signet ring hit my teeth through my cheek. Then he back-handed me, and the ring just missed my eye. Silent. Nothing Mrs. Morris would have heard. "God, Dad, stop hitting me!"

"Shut up. You just want that old black bitch to come over here."

"He's beating me. I'm serious." I was yelling straight at the wall, hoping she was in the right part of the house. My whole head hurt. It wasn't just that I'd been hit. I'd been slammed.

My father hollered at the wall, too. "He's just trying to get me in trouble, Mrs. Morris. Ignore him."

"Call 911. He's going to kill me. He's got a gun."

The doorbell rang. I was glad it did, because I was regretting saying he had a gun. Even someone as no-nonsense as Mrs. Morris would have been crazy to come to a house where there was a gun.

My father opened the door, and the first thing Mrs. Morris said was, "Son, don't go telling people your daddy's got a gun on you. Nobody's going to come running if there's a gun."

In spite of myself, I gave her a little smile. She took one look at my face and knew it was a good thing she'd come over.

"He's got Attention Deficit Disorder," my father said. "He's very hard to control."

Mrs. Morris didn't let him catch her eye, didn't let him play that "we're-the-adults" game. She looked at me. "Do you need me to call Child Protective Services?" she said.

My hand automatically went up to my face. My father said to me, "Don't pull that bullshit." Then he said to Mrs. Morris, "Everything is all right over here. I promise you."

"Look, I know a thing or two. You think I don't know child abuse when I see it? The only difference with a white child is that it shows up better in a photo."

My father got very quiet. I understood what she was saying, so I knew he did, too. Mrs. Morris had him. She could evict him. She could get him sent to jail. Thank goodness I had a real home, or she could have had me put into foster care, not that that mattered to my father.

"This won't happen again," my father said, finally. "If it means Otto won't come over for a while, that's what will have to happen."

I instantly was sorry I'd hollered.

Mrs. Morris thought that one over for a while. Finally, she said, "If I hear one sound tonight, I'm not ringing the doorbell. No. I'm dialing 911 directly." Then she walked out the door.

CHAPTER SIX

I was dreaming that Coach Jorge was my dad. He was bossing me around, making me pick up all the equipment in the gym after the other kids had gone home, and I was really happy. It was like getting in on a secret, being there and seeing what it was like when all the overhead lights were off, finding out that Coach was the same in real life as in school life. He knew I liked helping, or he wouldn't have given me all those jobs.

My father woke me up, and it was funny because he sounded a lot like Coach Jorge in the dream. Not the voice, of course, because Coach had an accent, but the niceness. "Hey, buddy, if you hurry, I'll get you McDonald's on the way."

I kept my eyes closed. I wasn't sure what was real. "What?" I said with my eyes still closed. A lot of times when I was really sleepy I didn't know where dreams ended.

My father actually sat next to me on the sofa. He put his hand on my shoulder. I could feel it. It was real. "Come on. McDonald's. I'll drive slowly so you can finish before you get to the gate."

That sounded very real. I rolled over, opened my eyes, stretched, and there was my same father. I thought

I saw a funny look on his face for a second, but it went away. "I've made your lunch and everything."

I kicked off the covers as well as I could, given that I had this man with a pretty big butt sitting next to me. He'd made my lunch one time before. It was this slice of baloney and a slice of yellow cheese on white bread with mayonnaise. That was it. I hadn't even found anybody I could trade with. He'd told me Grandmama Fisher had made him that sandwich every day when he was in fourth grade. I'd asked him what she'd made in fifth grade, and he'd said, "Actually, tuna fish, and she never drained it, just added mayonnaise. My bag was really leaky, but it sure tasted good."

Looking back, I was grateful he'd missed my point.

I felt a little sorry for him right then, making a sandwich nobody was going to eat. I told him thanks, and I hurried to get dressed. I'd find a way to save my McDonald's for lunch.

I was a little early for school. I always was on the days my father drove me. Most of the time now, I'd stay over on nights when my mother didn't have carpool. She got a break those mornings, though that didn't occur to my father. All he knew was that he didn't have to have her sitting in front of his house proving to him that she was smarter than him.

I didn't have to talk in the car because my mouth was full of bacon, egg, cheese, and biscuit. He even let me have Coke, because I was going to be the school's problem. I was wondering what he was going to say when we drove up to the gate. I'd brushed my teeth. I'd seen what I looked like in the mirror. I'd realized why my father had looked at me funny when I woke up. If he'd had any sense, he'd have kept me home. I didn't think he could have taken me to his office, and I wasn't sure he could have taken me back to my mother, but he sure shouldn't have taken me to school. I was expecting Mrs. Barber to open the car door to let me out and for her to say, "What on earth happened to you?" and then to look at my father. If that didn't happen, at least I wondered what he was going to say to me. He'd told Mrs. Morris I wasn't coming back.

Just my luck, Mrs. Barber wasn't at the gate. An eighth-grade girl was doing gate duty while Mrs. Barber was back by the door, talking all seriously to a parent. "Whoa, Otto!" the girl said. I turned to my father to see what he'd say to me. "I'll give you a call," he said. "You take good care of yourself." He handed me a five-dollar bill.

If anybody called that eighth-grade girl to testify in court about my father, she'd have had to say that my father sounded very loving. If anybody called me to testify, I'd have had to say the same thing.

The first thing I did before going to my homeroom was slip into the boys' bathroom to look in the mirror. The mirrors in boys' bathrooms aren't very clear, because no boy in his right mind would be caught dead checking himself out, but I could see my face well enough. Both sides looked pretty bad. The right side was red and purple, and I thought I was getting a black eye. I thought it looked like a handprint, but that was probably because I knew what hit me. The left side wasn't as bad, but if I was on a forensic TV show like *CSI*, it had good evidence.

Even in the foggy mirror I could see a little square in the middle of the red, and in the middle of the square was what looked a lot like the letter "D" that I'd always liked to look at on my father's signet ring. A detective couldn't get anything better than that. I hoped somebody had a cell phone and would take my picture.

I had ten minutes before the bell, so I ran over to the gym. I still kind of had the dream in my brain, like Coach was my real father, not the father who gave me away, but the father I lived with. I wasn't going to say anything, because the truth was that I felt a little sorry for my Fisher father, but if somebody discovered he'd hit me, then it wasn't my fault the truth got out.

Coach was in the gym. I waved at him. "Hey," he hollered from across the gym, "you need something?" I got closer. I told him nothing was going on. I just thought I'd drop by. He told me I needed to get to class, but he said it in a fatherly way. He was busy bending over checking the floor. He always acted like he owned that floor. You weren't supposed to walk on it unless you wore sneakers. I realized I wasn't in my P.E. shoes. "Watch the floor," he said. "How about socks 'til you hit the door?"

He hadn't noticed my face at all.

By lunchtime, not one person had said a word to me about my face. A couple of people had stopped for a second or two to check me out, but they hadn't said anything. I thought Mrs. Phipps would be the one. She'd looked at me hard when she did the attendance roll, but then she went on down the alphabet. Mrs. Phipps should have known everything. I was sure I wasn't the first kid who'd come to St. Michael's all beaten up. Being rich didn't guarantee that kids had good parents. In fact, I bet fathers were meaner when they had more money. Probably the only difference with me was that my father was too dumb to keep me home.

Ren sat next to me at lunch. Just my luck. But I had a feeling he did it on purpose. Ren never acted all psychological because he went to a shrink, and in return nobody ever acted like he had to be crazy. Still, I probably wasn't the only person who had a feeling Ren was easy to talk to because he talked to a paid grownup. Nobody else ever talked to grownups, paid or unpaid.

"I can tell what happened to you," he whispered to me. I just opened my eyes wide at him, like I was saying, *Oh, yeah? What happened?* He leaned over and whispered in my ear, almost like a girl. "Your dad did that to your face."

I was sitting there with that stupid baloney sandwich and three bites of biscuit and a whole morning of people pretending nothing had happened to me, and here was my friend being good to me, and the only thing I could think to do was run out of the lunchroom before I started crying in front of the whole seventh grade.

I ran out onto the patio, but the third graders were out there playing. I ran back into the building, but I couldn't run into a classroom, because I didn't want a teacher to ask me what was wrong. If a teacher couldn't look at my face and ask what was wrong, then to hell with all the teachers. Finally, I ran into the bathroom. I didn't know Ren was behind me, and so was Michael. Michael didn't go to a psychiatrist, but he was a good friend. He was always in as much trouble as I was. The only difference was that both his parents loved him to death. Nobody else was in the bathroom.

"I'll stand lookout," Michael said, and he posted himself in the doorway, making sure any third-grader who needed to pee would just have to live with it.

"Hey, man, I'm sorry," Ren said.

I told him there was no need to apologize. Then I started getting angry, which was very good because it keeps a person from crying. "Do you know I've been walking around this school all day with my face like this, and not one teacher has said a word?"

"Why don't you just tell?" Ren asked.

"I don't want to get my dad in trouble," I said, and then I started laughing. Ren and Michael laughed, too, probably with relief.

Michael asked me what my mom said. "You think she's seen this?" I said. "Just wait until I get home today. I don't know who she'll be madder at, my dad or the school."

"Probably your dad," Ren said.

When we got back to the table, we took the baloney sandwich apart, piece by piece, then threw it away. They thought it was funny, and I tried to pretend it was, too. But somehow it still made me sad.

It was cold, but my mother was waiting out front when carpool dropped me off. She'd never done that before, not even when I was in fifth grade and she'd had to have our dog put to sleep while I was at school. This was weird. I couldn't imagine what was wrong, but I knew something was. I tried to act all cool, because the carpool had some younger kids in it, in fact only one other person my age, and she was a girl. Thank goodness the mom who was driving pulled off as soon as I got out of the car. Moms were supposed to wait until you got safely into the house, but as long as my mother was there, she figured I was all right. My mother ran up and threw her arms around me and hugged me and didn't let go. She was wearing a coat, and it was a pretty terrific hug. The coat made her bigger. Kind of fluffier.

I asked her what was wrong when she let me go, and she held my hand with both of her hands and led me into the house without saying anything. She looked so sad that I just knew somebody was dead. I didn't want to know. I didn't want to hear. Her hands were cold. She'd been waiting for me for a while. She led me to the sofa. "You want a snack? I bet you're hungry."

I'd been starving on my way home. I'd had Fritos and Kit Kats at lunch, using the five dollars, but they'd only made my stomach growl by 1:30. Now I wasn't hungry at all. I was scared. I didn't want to hear. I told her to please just tell me and get it over with.

"Mrs. Phipps called me this afternoon."

That was not anything like what I expected. "What?" I had no idea what she was talking about. I definitely wasn't in trouble. That wasn't the way things worked when I got into trouble. Someone from the office called when I was in trouble.

"Oh, sweetie, look at your face," she said. She reached out and touched my right cheek so lightly I could barely feel it, but her fingers were still cold, and what I felt was good. I didn't realize that my face hurt.

She didn't do a very good job of keeping herself from

crying, but she did a good job of explaining to me that in fact everybody at school sure had noticed what my father had done to me. Coach had seen it, Mrs. Phipps had seen it, even the headmaster had made a point of seeing it when he heard about it. Mrs. Phipps had called my mother because she was upset. She knew my mother couldn't possibly know. And she knew when my mother saw it she was going to wonder why in hell—*those were her exact words,* my mother said with a little smile—nobody at St. Michael's had called Child Protective Services.

Right at that moment Ada came slamming in from school, with Finn right behind her.

"What the hell happened to you?" she said when she saw me, without knowing or caring what was going on between me and my mother.

Finn walked up behind her. "Some jerk got you coming and going," he said. "You want me to beat the living shit out of him?" He realized where he was. "Oh, God, I'm so sorry, Mrs. Fisher."

It took my mother a second to realize that he was apologizing for saying "shit" in front of her. "Ada's father's moved out," my mother said. "New vocabulary rules in the house." She gave him a smile with her lips closed, not because she didn't just love Finn like crazy, but because she was having a hard time right then.

"You need us to get out of here?" Ada asked.

"Kind of," I said.

It was hard for my mother to get back to what we were talking about. She had lost some of her anger. I was kind of glad, because I was always afraid I was going to get kicked out of St. Michael's, and if they messed up, and she complained, that would give them a good reason.

"Mrs. Phipps said that the law requires them to call CPS if they suspect child abuse," my mother told me.

"And they suspected it," I said. I could imagine the headmaster looking for me. He knew who I was. I'd been there long enough.

"But they kind of have their own policy, see?" she said. I didn't say anything. I knew St. Michael's was different from other schools. For starters, there were probably very few other schools where kids in seventh grade wore short pants in spring. Or rode in carpools. Parents paid probably ten thousand dollars a year for the privilege of having their kids live with strange policies. "Their policy is to let the families work out their own problems. Most families can afford professional help."

"So jail is only for poor people," I said.

"That's what they think at St. Michael's."

I sort of felt relieved, because sending my father to jail would only make him sad and furious and poor. And he'd never come home. I looked my mother in the eye to see if I could tell whether she agreed with me.

"I'm not so sure what I think," she said.

Finn stayed for dinner. Since my father moved out, we'd been having meals that made Ada happy because she said she wanted to live by what she called the "eyelash rule": she didn't want to eat anything with eyelashes, because she could look into its eyes. My mother had been cooking red beans and rice from scratch with no pork, sockeye salmon that she said didn't have mercury in it, and that night we were having baked chicken, even though I secretly thought chickens had feelings.

"So what happened to you, man?" Finn said.

I looked to my mother. I really wanted to tell.

The phone rang. "Let it go," my mother said. Ada didn't care. She had a cell. I didn't care since it was never for me. We could hear the answering machine pick up in the kitchen. My parents had never switched over to voice mail. At the sound of the beep a voice said, "Hey, this is Ren…"

I jumped up from the table without permission and ran for the phone. I grabbed the portable and closed myself off in the laundry room. "Hey," I said while he was delivering some message that probably needed to be cut off.

"Whew," he said. "For a minute I thought you weren't there. Like maybe you'd gone back to your dad's house."

"I may be stupid, but I'm not dumb."

"You're not stupid," he said. "School's stupid."

Ren was probably the best person in the whole school. Everybody liked him. I never knew why I got to be his friend. "You didn't tell, did you?"

"Well, I told my psychiatrist," he said. "But he's bound by law not to tell anybody. Not even if I'm dead. Not even if somebody comes to him with a court order, I think, but I'm not sure."

I should have known that. I'd watched enough cop shows. But at least I knew I was probably safe. I asked Ren what the shrink said. Of course, I didn't call him a shrink. That would have been an insult to Dr. Klinger. I'd never insult Dr. Klinger.

"He said, 'Why didn't the school call Child Protective Services?' and I said I didn't know, but St. Michael's is very fancy, so maybe that's why. He was kind of hinting that he was under some obligation to call them, but I told him he couldn't."

"My father could go to jail."

Ren told me that he spent his whole session talking about that, about a kid being afraid of his father, about how he wasn't ever afraid of his, about imagining what it was like to be me, how sending your dad to jail might be worse than letting him run around and hit you, but then maybe it wasn't. "He said you probably wanted your dad back, and I asked him how he knew that, because it sounded weird, and he said he just figured."

I realized then I needed to see a shrink because he was right—I did want my dad back, even after last night. I also realized that seeing a shrink was never going to happen. My father thought it was too expensive for me to go to the pediatrician every few months to get Adderall.

When I got back to the table, they hadn't changed the subject. Because my mother was keeping it a secret about what had happened to me, Ada was extra curious, and she was trying to play Twenty Questions. "Was it a boy?" "Does he go to St. Michael's?"

Ada stared at me hard. It was dark outside, and the only light was from the wrought-iron chandelier over the table, so she got out of her chair and came over to stare at me up close. "I thought that mark on your face looked funny. Come look at this," she said to Finn.

They were both standing over me, breathing in my face, keeping me from eating while my food was still a little warm, and then Ada said, "I knew it! See that? It's that ugly old ring. Look. See? 'D'. You can't miss it. Mama, are you insane?"

My mother kept eating, but she was taking very small

bites and pushing her food around a lot. Finally, she said, "I really don't know what to do."

Ada blew up like it was the big moment she'd been waiting for her entire life. "You don't know what to do?" She wasn't mad at Mom, but she sure was mad. "Here's what you do. You take a picture for court." She turned to Finn. "Go get my cell. No, wait, go get yours. It's better. We'll do it in the bathroom where there's good light. Right now, when it looks like he's been half killed." She turned back to my mother. "Then you call the authorities." She looked at me. "Get up. Don't worry. It's not like you see on *Cops*. They're not going to come take you in the night and put you in a foster home. You're already home. They'll haul him off to jail, and you'll just be sitting right here, nice as you please, and he'll finally get what he deserves."

I didn't get up. I was hungry. The mark wasn't going to go away in ten minutes.

Ada turned to my mother, who had finally put her fork down. "He beat the crap out of all of us. And we never did anything about it. Don't you think it's time he got what he deserved?"

A big smile came across Ada's face. Everyone waited for what was coming. "I'm just imagining," she said. "Can you picture that fat old slob, sitting in prison with all those hardened criminals? They'll beat the crap out of him. Especially since you know that in a mostly black city, you've got mostly black guys in prison. They'll smell racism all over him. Oh, boy, is this great." That was the line we always used from Flounder in *Animal House*. But usually it was funny.

I was looking down at the chicken on my plate and

thinking about that baloney sandwich, and that poor fat guy who made that sandwich, and I thought about how maybe there was another way to fix him besides prison, but I wasn't going to go up against Ada when she had so much right to be angry since he'd never made her a sandwich, probably, and then my mother said, "Honey, it's not that simple."

"I don't care," Ada said.

"He'll lose tenure," my mother said. I didn't know what tenure was, but it obviously was something complicated that my mother had been thinking about a lot.

Ada said she didn't care. Let him lose his job. Let him have to try to find work someplace else after he'd had tenure at Tulane. Everybody'd want to know why he'd leave Tulane when they'd given him tenure. I figured that meant something good enough to keep him there forever. Let him wind up having to teach seventh grade, Ada said. Dr. Fisher teaching seventh grade. See how well he'd do at that. Ada was going wild with her fantasies of our father's downfall after the years in prison she was sure he'd get for smacking me across the face twice.

"He's paying child support," my mother said.

"I'm sure as soon as I turn eighteen, he'll cut it in half," Ada said.

"There's still your brother."

Ada was still standing over me. I was hunched over, trying to eat my chicken. I was kind of nauseated, but I had to do something. "Oh, God, Mama." Ada sounded sorry, but sorry about my mother, not about me. Which was fine with me. Somehow I wasn't seeing myself as the victim at that very moment. "He really has you believing you need him."

"This is a big house."

"I bet what he'll give you is about what you get for a vase."

My mother got the most amazing expression on her face, like someone had just told her that for the next hour everything she touched would turn to gold. "Well, maybe a vase and a bowl," she said.

"And who knows how to use the power drill?" Ada asked. She folded her arms and leaned back, with this look of admiration that said, *You don't need a husband.*

My mother smiled.

"So I'm calling the police," Ada said.

"Wait!" I said.

If my life had been a movie, everybody would have stopped in their tracks and looked at me and realized, *Oh, wow, this is all about Otto. We forgot about Otto, and we need to find out what he wants and then do it.* But the closest my life came to a movie was to *Radio Flyer*, which was always my dream movie because I could make believe that if my father beat me up too much, I could fly away on a wagon or something and escape. And that means my life wasn't close to any movie. Which means that nobody heard me say, "Wait!"

Ada pulled me out of my chair to get me into the bathroom for my photo. But Finn just stood where he was until Ada told him to go get his cell phone. My mother said, "I think I need to be the one to call the police. And definitely we can't call 911. This isn't an emergency." She went running to the kitchen for the phone book, while Ada was saying into her phone, "Police, non-emergency." She used her paycheck to get a cell phone upgrade every time a new one came along.

I was finally stronger than my sister. She'd been bigger than me my whole life, but the time had finally come when I was taller and heavier. I quit letting her pull me. And without being mean at all, I gently pulled her cell phone away from her. I wasn't sure if she was asking for a phone number or making a call, but I wasn't taking any chances.

"What's wrong with you?" she said.

"I said, 'Wait.'"

Ada folded her arms in front of her and stared right at me. "I don't get it."

I stared right back at her. "You never asked me what I wanted to do." She gave me a look I'd seen a lot in my life. This time it was saying, *You're only thirteen. Of course I didn't ask you.*

"I feel a little sorry for Dad."

"Don't call him Dad."

"Maybe you not talking to him is enough punishment," I said.

"Ha!" Ada said, but it was a phony "ha!" "He doesn't even know I'm alive. Which of course is because I stay below his radar. And that's kind of pitiful, if you ask me. I mean, most kids would tell their parents when they make valedictorian. But if I tell him, then he'll know I'm applying to Brown, and he'll attack me." She didn't take one breath. She was getting red in the face.

Finn came over and put his arm around her shoulder.

She put her arms around his waist and leaned her head on his chest. I felt kind of stupid standing there. Well, maybe not stupid. More like alone.

"I think a kid needs a dad," I said. I was sure I knew that.

Ada didn't say anything. My mother was in the doorway, holding the phone book, just watching, hoping, probably, that we would figure out what she was going to do. Finally, Finn said, "Yeah, every kid needs a dad. But it might not be your *father*."

I didn't get it. I just looked at him.

He got this kind of fake smile on his face, but I didn't hold it against him, because he was a very good guy. "Hey, look. Ada says you need a basketball coach. Want me to come? I'm center on the Newman team. You ever want to go to the skateboard rink up off Carrollton? I'll drop you off and pick you up. You can hang with the guys, how about it?"

When I was little, it was easy to buy me off with chocolate. This was a whole bag of Hershey kisses. I gave him a very smart grin. "So what's the trade?" I asked.

"No trade," he said. "I've got Ada right here. Your mom's going to handle your father." He looked at Ada. "Right? Father." Ada looked up at him. Ada would do anything Finn told her to do. Lucky for Ada, Finn would only tell her to do the right things.

CHAPTER SEVEN

My mother made her decision. She hadn't talked to anyone but herself. Overnight, with very little sleep. She announced it to Ada and me before we left for school on Monday morning, and that was probably the first small step in her strategy. We didn't have time to argue. Not that I would have. It worked for me. It gave my father another chance. Which means it didn't work for Ada. She had photos of me in her phone, and she was going to go to Walgreens after school for multiple prints, and my father wasn't getting any more chances. She was expecting to be prepared for interviews with dumb social workers she could out-talk. She was expecting prosecutors who would say she was their dream witness. My mother's plan didn't work for her.

My mother planned to take either or both of us over to my father's house and tell him "in no uncertain terms" that he was in deep trouble, and she could file for a divorce, and what was he going to do about his children and also about his problem as an abuser? She wouldn't call authorities if he showed remorse, which meant he was truly sorry. This was "make it or break it" time. She was going over to tell him to earn his way back. If he wanted.

Ada flew out of the house, saying, "You're a victim, Mama. Please don't keep being a victim. Abusers always apologize."

I went out the door saying, "He's probably really sad."

There is no way to know exactly what happened when she phoned my father during the school day. But Ada got a lot out of her. She said we should have been proud of her, because he wanted to meet that very afternoon, and she refused, saying that she was sure Otto wanted to come, and everybody knew that Otto wasn't at his best after school. Of course, I'm sure my father had said, *Yes, give me a little sympathy here. None of this would have happened if I hadn't had the damn kid in the afternoon when he's so impossible.* Or something like that. Then he'd wanted Saturday so he could get it over with, and my mother had reminded him that she worked at RHINO some Saturdays, and this was one when she was on the schedule. Naturally, he'd referred to her pottery as her "little hobby," which had made Ada explode because, even though we didn't know exactly how much money either of our parents earned, we were pretty sure our mother earned as much as our father.

"All he's good for is health insurance," Ada hollered. "And who's ever heard of him outside of Tulane? You get written up in *Gambit* and the *Times-Picayune* all the time. And even *Southern Living.* Your stuff is going to be in people's houses long after you're dead."

"Thanks a lot," my mother had said.

"He doesn't sound like somebody who knows he's in deep shit," Ada said.

"Trust me, he does," my mother said.

Ada leaned over and gave her a big, sweet kiss on the cheek.

I dressed like I was going to church. I only went to church when my school had events like on Christmas Eve, because my parents just chose to ignore religion and my mother was really Jewish, but I wore a nice long-sleeved, blue oxford-cloth shirt and a navy cashmere vest and khaki slacks. I combed my hair really neatly. My mother didn't do anything special. She was ready to go into her studio as soon as we went back home. I knew both of us had thought hard about our clothes.

My father hadn't seen me in almost a week, and the marks on my face had turned to bruises that were somewhat fading to yellow, but still looked pretty awful. The rest of me looked terrific, I thought, and when he saw me at the door, I swear he had tears in his eyes. I felt my mother's hand on my shoulder as we walked into his front room. He really had the heat cranked up nicely, and there was a plate of those really good cookies from Whole Foods on the table. "I got Celestial Seasonings decaf for you, Elise," he said. "Make yourselves comfortable. Want to try hazelnut decaf coffee?" he asked me.

I nodded. I didn't feel so good.

He was gone for a few minutes, and at first neither of us said anything. Finally, I whispered, "I think he wants us to like him." My mother just nodded. I realized it was a stupid thing to say.

"So!" he said when he sat down with his coffee just like

mine. He even had Splenda for my mother. I wondered if maybe he was trying to get her to not divorce him.

"I'd like this to be a social visit," my mother said, "but I'm afraid it isn't."

My father looked at me. "I'm thinking Otto and I can work out temporary visitation, so I would hope this is a good place to start."

My mother put down her tea. She hadn't touched the cookies, so I hadn't, either. Which was too bad, because they were those really good cookies. Whole Foods used the best ingredients, which was why they could charge $14.95 for eight.

"I'm afraid visitation is about the last thing you can be asking for. It was all I could do the other night to keep Ada from calling the police." My mother thought for a second, then said, "Really, it was all I could do to keep *myself* from calling the authorities."

"Look, okay, I hit him too hard, but it's not exactly a crime. Hey, Otto, I told you I was sorry, didn't I?"

"Actually, you didn't." As soon as the words were out, I felt bad that I'd said them. But I couldn't take them back.

His lips made a straight line. Back at home, it would have meant to shut the hell up if I knew what was good for me. "I think getting you McDonald's is a pretty good apology."

"I think getting him McDonald's is just getting the kid breakfast, and a pretty lousy excuse for breakfast at that," my mother said.

"Are we going to get all semantic here?" my father said. "He knew I was sorry, okay? No big deal."

"The headmaster of the school thought what you did to his face was a damn big deal."

"If he'd been in public school like I wanted, there wouldn't have been any fancy-pants headmaster."

"No," my mother said, "there would have been a principal who'd have called Child Protective Services as soon as he walked in through the gate. St. Michael's likes to let families work things out themselves. Which is what I thought I'd try to do."

My father took that in. "So I apologized. What more can I do?" My father sounded like he had no clue.

"Think," my mother said.

I smiled a little inside. That was what my father called the Socratic method. He wouldn't tell me anything if I asked for help. He'd say, "Think." But only when he knew the answer.

"Don't pull that bullshit on me," he said.

My mother sat up straight. I'd never seen her act like that before. Like she had some kind of power. "You want me to walk out of here?" she said. "I have options. I'm trying to give you a chance."

At that my father did something I hoped I'd never see again. He burst into tears. It was truly sickening. He turned all pink, and tears came out of his eyes for real, and he sobbed like a little kid. I'd never seen that happen before, and I was so embarrassed I'd have done anything to make it stop. I went over and put my arm around his shoulder. I didn't feel sorry for him any more than I had the other day at school when I was throwing away my lunch. I sure didn't feel sorry for him for crying. But I needed to make him stop crying. I thought if he didn't stop, I would lose my mind. That was all I could think, that I would lose my mind. He had his face in his hands, and his shoulders were shaking. I could feel it all through my body. Not just his shaking, but the feeling that I was going to stop being in the world.

"Hey, hey," my mother said all gently. "I'm sorry. I know this must be rough. Usually, it's supposed to be harder on the one who gets left, but I'm sure you're having trouble with moving out."

My father looked up, and I stepped away. He'd stopped sobbing for the most part. I was back to having a little hope that the regular Otto could stand to be himself.

"Oh, honey, I want to come back home," he said to my mother.

I wanted to jump up and hug him. My mother didn't say anything, but her face said, *What?*

"I miss you so much," my father said. He was talking to my mother and sounding a little mushy, and I was back to wanting to escape being Otto again. I said I was going to the kitchen. My mother grabbed my hand and told me not to worry.

"Elise, I need you," he said.

"I came over here to talk about Otto," my mother said. She was still holding my hand. Usually, you don't hold your mother's hand when you're thirteen, but I sure needed to hang on. Maybe she'd feel my message, *Let him come home.*

"But we're a family," he said.

My mother thought for a few seconds. She was an artist, and he was a man who played with words all day for a living, and besides, he was crazy, and I felt sorry for her, because she was going to get tricked. "Right now you and I are married, living separately, and we have two children together, and we need to figure out what you can and cannot do with one of them," she said.

"You're forgetting our other child," he said.

Oh, that sounded kind of insane.

"Your other child will be eighteen in March and wants nothing to do with you."

"My other child will be going to college and needs me."

My mother's hand started to squeeze mine. I knew she was getting frustrated. I squeezed back. "I'm here to talk about Otto," she said, again.

"I had you over to talk about getting back together," he said. "It's the best thing for everyone. Having Otto over here overnight doesn't work at all."

"It really sucks," I said. I was on his side.

"This is none of your business," he said.

I stood up and said I wanted to go home. I was still holding my mother's hand. She pulled on my hand to have me sit down. It didn't take much. I was on her side, now.

"Listen, mister," she said to my father, "you need professional help. Psychiatric, not just marriage counseling. Until you've done some serious changing, you're only seeing this kid in public places. Got it?"

"People in my family don't see shrinks," he said.

"*Res ipsa loquitur*," my mother said. She turned to me. "That means, 'the thing speaks for itself.'" I figured that meant that you could look at how crazy they were and tell they never got any help from psychiatrists.

"Well, I don't see any point in your plan," my father

said. My mother looked confused. "If I can't live with him, I'm not taking him out for dinner."

"Suit yourself," my mother said, and she started to stand up.

My father started crying again.

My mother took one look at him, and I could just see that his crying did something different to her than it did to me. It made her soft and motherly. If I was honest, it made me a little disgusted. "Oh, God, I'm sorry," my mother said. "You really miss the kids, don't you?"

My father nodded. This time his face wasn't in his hands, and I could see his tragic-looking face with all the tears. It was pitiful. I wondered if he'd ever cried in front of my mother before.

"Listen, we'll work something out, all right? What about just starting out with taking Otto to dinner, see how that goes? Get to know him. Without any responsibility? What do you think?"

My father nodded again.

I hated to think what Ada was going to say. The subject of divorce hadn't even come up.

CHAPTER EIGHT

As it turned out, Ada had bigger things on her mind. We came home from my father's house and found her and Finn sitting in the living room looking like they were waiting for us. Like they were really nervous to find out how things went.

"You've been waiting for us?" my mother asked. She didn't sit down.

"I really don't give a shit about Otto's father," Ada said. "If that's what you're thinking."

Finn scooched up closer to Ada on the sofa and looked at my mother. "It'd probably be better if Otto went into his room," he said very nicely.

"I don't care what Otto hears," Ada said. "Otto's had a more complicated life than people three times his age. Stay," she said to me. "You're old enough to know about this."

"Oh, God," my mother said. I had a feeling my mother knew what was going on. I didn't have a clue. "Otto, maybe you better not listen." I didn't know how she could figure out anything from almost no clues, but then my mother watched more reality TV than even I did.

"Hey!" Ada said. "Otto probably understands more than any of us. He's the one who's adopted."

"Oh, shit, I'm right," my mother said. I still didn't have a clue. "Today is too hard," my mother whispered. She looked really pale, like she might pass out.

"It's okay," Ada said. "I've got it all figured out."

I didn't know what they were talking about. I asked if somebody would please tell me what was going on. It was obviously really important.

"I'm having a baby," Ada said.

"Wow," I said. That was terrific.

"She means she's pregnant," my mother said. "When you're pregnant, having a baby is just one thing that might happen."

I said that I thought having a baby would be awesome. In a split second I'd assumed it would be a little boy. I'd be kind of like a young dad to it.

"Finn and I have thought this out," Ada said. She was annoyed at my mother.

My mother asked her how long she'd known. Ada said, long enough. My mother said she needed to be more specific. This was boring the hell out of me. Even Maury Povich didn't fool with this kind of information, and he dealt in DNA on his show. Then my mother started in on Plan B versus something called RU 486, which I could tell were ways to get rid of a baby.

"How do you know this stuff?" I asked. I was really disgusted. Why would my mother, of all people, know about killing babies?

"Everybody knows that crap," Ada said. "They probably teach it in every school except Newman. At

Newman they figure you wouldn't dare get pregnant. Of course everybody does, and everybody has a friend who knows something, so why waste valuable class time?"

I couldn't believe nobody at Newman ever had a baby. Ada said that, oh, yes, some girl did back in the 90s, but she was like Ada. She was due in the summer, so she just went ahead and finished the school year, and nobody did anything about it. That's what Ada planned to do.

"And then what?" my mother said.

"I'll go to goddamn Tulane," Ada said, sounding very much like someone who was announcing that she was willing to pay a million dollars ransom for something. I still didn't understand, exactly.

"What about you, Finn?" my mother asked. Finn was planning to go to college up north near Brown, if not to Brown. He and Ada were both so smart that they were only applying to Ivy League colleges and Tulane. From what Ada made sure to tell my father, Newman's policy was always to aim as high as you could, and then to apply to Tulane for safety, because Tulane never turned down anybody from Newman. People who went to Newman said that going to Tulane was like repeating Newman ninth grade for four years, drinking yourself sick, and getting a degree.

Finn said he'd go to Tulane. Even I could hear the sadness in his voice.

"You can't ruin Finn's life," my mother said to Ada.

Ada looked at Finn, really looked at him. She didn't say anything.

My mother waited for the silence to get to all of us. Then she said, "I'm going to buy Plan B. It's supposed to be good for only three days, but you've really got up to two weeks. Okay?"

Ada nodded.

I wanted to say that they couldn't kill my new baby, but I didn't.

That was one good thing about ADHD. I never got worried about any one thing for any longer than it took for me to notice it and walk away. There were a couple of things that weren't changing, and every day I'd realize it a couple of times, and at those times I'd get all jumpy, but then I'd walk into another room and think about something else.

I wasn't going to my father's house, and he wasn't working anything out with my mother about me. I noticed that every day when I came home from school. *Whew, good!* I'd think, and I'd be a little disappointed and a little sad, but mostly I'd be relieved that I didn't have to fight, and I'd head for the refrigerator and fix a snack. I might think about my father's sorry excuse for a refrigerator while I was making a lot of good choices, but then I'd get my plate piled up and head for the TV.

That's when the other piece of worry would get my attention.

My mother had gone to Walgreens just as she said she would. And she'd bought the Plan B just as she said she would. It was in a Walgreens bag, which I didn't touch. I wasn't scared of it, like it would hurt me some kind of way. I just didn't want to move it because I didn't want my mother to think Ada had done anything with it and changed her mind. I tried to keep a mental count of the days since it was bought. Which made no sense because I didn't know how long that two weeks had been running. Every afternoon it was still there. It began to feel like it had been two weeks, but I couldn't tell. I hoped it had been. The longer Ada waited, the more chance there was that she was going to stay pregnant. It wasn't that I was like some girl who wanted to play baby dolls. I just wanted a little kid who I could be really nice to. I definitely would play basketball with him.

That day the bag was gone. I ran into my mother's studio. "Ada took the pills," I said.

My mother was working at the potter's wheel. She couldn't stop at that very second, but she told me to hold on, give her a minute. I stood by and watched. I didn't think I'd ever get tired of seeing what she could do with clay. Something from nothing. It soothed me.

She let the wheel slow down to a stop, but didn't wipe off her hands. I knew that meant we were just going to talk for a few minutes. "I took it back to Walgreens," she said. "It's too late."

I tried not to smile, but she saw me.

"That just means that if she decides to terminate, it's going to be very painful and expensive," she said.

"Or maybe she might have it."

My mother held her arms wide, her clay-covered hands reaching out like she was going to say some prayer about her studio. "I can't have a baby in this house."

"Oh."

If Ada didn't live in our house, I wouldn't be the big brother. It wouldn't do any good if she and Finn got an apartment and went to Tulane. That would be like me getting visitation rights or something. Unless I moved in with them. And if my father could only afford a half-double where I slept on a ratty sofa, then Ada and Finn weren't going to do much better. In fact, they probably were going to do a lot worse.

"I'd keep him out of your studio," I said.

"Right. You and Ada go to school all day, and I'm here with a baby and, you know, babies start to walk, and I'm here to tell you that a baby in this studio is a serious mess." Her eyes got extra wide and her mouth formed an "O" and she looked at me like she was saying, *You were one hell of a baby, Otto.*

"You can't kill a baby," I said.

She held her arms up in the air. "I can't hug you, but you can hug me, please," she said. It was her way of knowing I was glad nobody had killed me. I went over and squeezed her tight.

I let her finish the vase. She couldn't kill the vase. That's how I saw it. I sat and watched. When she washed her hands, we could go eat and talk, and then she could explain. She said this was all personal, that neither one of us was pregnant, but both of us had to have a private choice, that both of us had to decide what to say to Ada. She told me that somehow pregnancies like Ada's were political, and when I said I didn't understand, she explained that a lot of people, most of them men who could never get pregnant, thought it was their business to say what women could do if they didn't want their pregnancies. I said I could understand. I wanted Ada's baby. "But you can't make her," my mother said. No, I couldn't.. And we took it from there.

"You have to understand," my mother said. "This is a hypothetical child." I didn't stop her. I got angry when my father used complicated words because he used them to make me feel bad. My mother used them because she assumed I understood. I figured I'd get it eventually if she talked long enough. I heard "pathetic" in the middle, but that probably wasn't a clue.

"You probably have imagined it already, huh?"

I smiled pretty happily. Ada and Finn had a lot in common, looks-wise. Both still had blondish hair even in twelfth grade, especially Ada, who put streaks in hers. And they both had greenish-bluish eyes, which I thought probably made my father pretty happy, because that meant Ada wasn't very Jewish-looking, even though a lot of the Jewish kids at St. Michael's also had light hair. Of course, the main thing I pictured about the baby was that it was a boy, and it already was about three, so it could try to throw a ball into a basket.

"Okay, so picture a child in your mind," my mother said. "Now, bear with me. Imagine what that child would be like if you and, say, Samantha, were boyfriend and girlfriend."

That sounded totally disgusting. So far, my taste in girls ran to choosing by personality, even if it was made-up personality. And I couldn't imagine going anywhere near Samantha's for-real personality.

My mother could see the expression on my face. "We're talking hypothetical here. You can pretend it happens in a test tube, okay?"

That was fine. I certainly wasn't going to tell her about Emma Watson and how good she was for poor old Harry Potter.

"So what kind of kid would you and Samantha have?"

"Anything's possible," I said. "But people with dark hair usually have kids with dark hair, even if they're married to somebody blond. Though most moms with blond hair dye it, anyway. But it definitely would have brown eyes. And it'd be a girl. Probably a snotty girl." Why was my mother doing this?

"That's a hypothetical baby right?" she said. I nodded. "Well, Ada's baby right now is completely hypothetical, too. An idea. Right now it's nothing more than what you might see in science class, just a little bit of stuff in a Petri dish, nothing you'd be upset about."

Like it was no big deal, my father called, and I went out to dinner that night with him, and I got him to lecture me about books because it was a safe plan. I walked in the front door all excited because I'd figured out how to fake it with him.

"So tell me about Dickens," was all I'd had to say. He'd told me stories that I'd zoned in and out of, and some parts had been a little interesting. I'd even remembered when it got quiet to say, "What about Pip?" Pip had almost been my name. That had been the story that got him really excited, probably, I thought, because Pip had been an orphan who was a lot worse off than I was. I figured he was going to tell me the whole book in pieces if I saw him more times. He said that was how Dickens sold his books, in small pieces, and people would wait for the pieces to come off the boat.

But my mother and Ada didn't care about me being friends with my father. Especially Ada. She actually had news that was more important.

"Mama explained to me that this baby is hypothetical," she said to me. That didn't sound like news. "So it's as real as a baby Finn and I could have if we, say, went to college and then got married."

That was true.

"Ada got her early admission letter today," my mother said. "I waited to show it to her until we talked."

I knew what an early admission letter was. Ada had been talking about it for months. She'd applied for early admission to Brown, and Finn hadn't. She absolutely wanted to go there, but Finn wanted to consider Harvard and Williams, too, so he applied for what was called regular admission. If Ada got early admission, she didn't have to worry about college the rest of the year.

"I think what you did was kind of a federal offense," Ada said to my mother. "But I'm kind of grateful you did it." She explained that she meant my mother hiding the mail.

I was completely confused. And the truth was that I didn't want to know that much about Ada's life. It was kind of boring. Being in twelfth grade had nothing to do with being in seventh grade. All that mattered to me was whether she was staying home and giving us a baby.

"So?" I asked.

"So, this isn't really a baby," Ada said. "I'm willing to wait. I really want to go to Brown."

"You're going to kill it," I said.

My mother reminded me that it was really just a little stuff in a Petri dish.

But I was once a little stuff. And the girl or woman

or whatever she was who got pregnant with me, she let me get my arms and legs and head and all and get born. "He's hypothetical, but he could be another me," I said.

"There's never going to be another you," my mother said.

She reminded me that even though she didn't have any particular spiritual life, she knew that she was at the agency at the exact right time to get the exact right child. "Children are born to get the right parents at the right time, I just know it," she said.

That sounded just a little more believable than Santa Claus and the Easter Bunny, but it was good enough for me. What counted was that my mother believed it. And if I thought about it, Samantha's mother was a total bitch, so they got matched up at the right time, too.

Ada stayed home the day she did the first part of the procedure. She wasn't eighteen yet, though she was close, so my mother had to be totally involved, but my mother said she would have been involved anyway, even if Ada had been eighty-eight. We all had laughed, picturing Ada as this skinny old woman with a belly like a basketball, using a walker, scooting along behind her hundred-and-something-year-old mother, who of course would have dyed hair. I wondered how many kids in my class knew about aborting babies and making jokes about them. Probably some of them knew just enough to be disgusting.

When I got home from school, Ada was all by herself on the sofa, looking miserable. Finn wasn't there, and she said it was her choice, that she didn't want him to see her like this. My mother was in the studio, but they both had cell phones. So I sat down with Ada and offered to get her a snack. "Get yourself one," she said. She always could read my mind.

She was all curled up on the sofa, her arms across her stomach, kind of the way she acted when she had a really bad period, which was too much information for me, but she never cared. I looked at her, and I said the first thing that came into my mind. "Dad ought to know about this."

"Are you out of your mind?" She was pissed.

"It's not what you're thinking," I said. If I didn't explain, she was going to throw me out of the room. When Ada was feeling like this, I knew better than to cross her.

"If that man knew about this, it'd give him one more reason to think I was a piece of crap."

That had never occurred to me. Ada was the good kid. Ada had just gotten early acceptance to just about the hardest college in the entire country. All the famous kids went to Brown. They used to go to Yale, she'd told me, but now Brown was the cool place to go. And Ada was extra cool because they took her early. Nobody could think Ada was crap.

"I was thinking he'd find out how much you're hurting, and he'd feel bad," I said.

Ada let out a little sob of pain. Then she whispered, "You're something else."

I really didn't have the right to be talking to somebody that much older than me. She was probably thinking I was dumb. I shrugged my shoulders. I needed to get out of there, but she was all by herself. The TV wasn't even on.

"I'm sorry," I said.

Ada smiled, and even though her lips were closed because she was hurting, I could tell she meant it. "Hey, talking to you is like talking to Finn," she said.

"Okay," I said. I couldn't believe it. "So, you know how, when something really hurts, like if you've got some cut and it's bleeding, if you're mad at somebody, you want them to see where you're cut, because they have to feel sorry for you, well, sorrier for you than for themselves, and they feel bad, kind of jealous or something, and you feel better?"

"God, I love you," Ada said.

"So, you want me to tell him?"

"Oh, no!"

I asked her why not.

"Because," she said, "the reason I'm hurting is that I did something that he'll say makes me deserve to be hurting. He'd probably say I deserve to hurt for the rest of my life."

"You did it on purpose?" I was feeling like Dr. Phil.

Ada didn't answer right away. Any talk show host would have jumped right on her and said that if she had to think about it, it probably meant that it wasn't strictly an accident. I of course knew how people got pregnant, and I knew about birth control, sort of, and I definitely knew about condoms because you had to know about condoms in seventh grade or people thought you were an idiot. But this was my sister, and I seriously did not want to know about her having sex. Like, if the condom broke, that would be way too much information. And if they decided just once to do it without protection, if she told me that, I would not be able to look her or Finn in the eye for a very long time.

"Wait, never mind," I said. "I shouldn't know the answer. I really shouldn't know the answer."

CHAPTER NINE

My father hated Mardi Gras. He had a dozen reasons why, and over my lifetime he let most of them out. "New Orleans has no middle class," he'd say. "So what you get out there are the stinking rich and the stinking poor." Sometimes my mother would point out that at least there were very few Jews, but he didn't think she was funny. Mardi Gras was idiotic, with the same floats with the same giant heads, every single year at every single parade, at least according to him. And he saw no reason in the world to catch beads. He didn't care about the environment, but he was willing to say that Mardi Gras beads surely were leaching lead into our drinking water. And public drunkenness was his favorite topic of all. Because he taught at Tulane, he was sure that the already-low IQs of his students dropped thirty points between freshman and senior years from alcohol consumption.

For my entire life, that had meant that the only way I saw parades was to spend the night at friends' houses. The only exception was my father's one excursion to see the Krewe duh Vieux. They made fun of everybody. And the year they made fun of Mayor Ray Nagin, my dad almost lost his mind with happiness. After Katrina, when the float rolled down the street with Nagin's big old head, my father whooped like a normal person.

This year Mardi Gras was going to be easy, I thought. My mother could drop me at the parade route and pick me up nearby when I called her using her cell. But I had a feeling my father actually planned to keep me from the parades, because he invited Grandmama Fisher to visit for two weeks, and the two weeks ran right through the parade schedule. I didn't know why she wanted to see me all the time she was in New Orleans, since she clearly had no use for a boy who wasn't related to her, but somehow she and my father knew when the best floats—Babylon, Endymion, and Bacchus—were rolling, and those were the nights we absolutely needed to have dinner together.

My father lived three blocks from St. Charles. That meant that every inch of space was parked up in his neighborhood. If he left his house, he wouldn't be able to come home until long after the street cleaners had passed on the avenue. Which meant that I had to be dropped off there to eat whatever Grandmama Fisher cooked. It also meant that I was trapped in that house with two against one. And the general noise in the city was so loud that I had a feeling Mrs. Morris wouldn't hear anything going on next door to her. Assuming she was home. I figured Mrs. Morris didn't go to parades. But it wasn't out of grumpiness like my father. She probably grew up in New Orleans and loved the floats and bands but felt like parades meant being in a circle of laughing friends. I'd never seen her with a lot of laughing friends. People probably didn't have very many after they got older. I knew Grandmama Fisher didn't, but then she and Mrs. Morris were pretty different.

We were sitting at the kitchen table, eating a casserole that I had to admit tasted really good. It was chili with a lot of ground meat and noodles and cheddar cheese. I could hear that funny mixed-up noise in the outside air that comes when a parade is passing. It's like a crowd is talking loud, not quite cheering, and a band is tuning up and not playing a song you can make out, but there's a drum beat to it. At regular times you could hear the streetcar passing from the kitchen. I was starving. The Adderall was wearing off. I really wanted to be at that parade. I didn't even need my friends, though I knew where some of them were. I'd even take Grandmama. I started eating fast. "You want to go to that parade?" I asked her.

"Do you know why we have Mardi Gras?" she asked.

I actually knew the answer. I went to an Episcopal school, after all. "It's right before Ash Wednesday," I said.

"That doesn't answer the question," my father said.

I was going to get cornered if I wasn't careful. I tried to think of a way to get the subject to Dickens, but I didn't know enough about Dickens.

"Well, it's French for Fat Tuesday, which means everybody celebrates, because then it's Ash Wednesday," I said.

"Everybody?" Grandmama asked. Her voice sure was twangy. A twangy voice has a way of sounding mean, no matter what.

I shrugged. I tried to think back to last year. There were almost no Catholics in St. Michael's, and I thought you had to be confirmed to get ashes, because three of the teachers got ashes, and I didn't know if Episcopalians got ashes, but definitely nobody else did. "Practically nobody goes for ashes at my school," I said.

"What about Easter?" Grandmama said. "Does anybody at your school have Easter?"

I nodded. Everybody at my school celebrated Easter, including the Jewish kids, I told her.

She looked at my father, like she'd hit the target. "You know you're supposed to be a Jew," she said to me. "I never know if I'm supposed to send you Christmas presents or not."

I didn't say anything. I knew better.

"Your mother is supposed to be making you a Jew. Are you having one of those bar mitzvahs?"

"Cut it out," my father said.

I still didn't say anything.

"I brought you into this world, I'll take you right out of it," she said to my father.

"I'm just asking you to lay off the Jewish stuff."

She looked at me. "Your daddy thinks I don't like Jews. I don't have a thing against Jews. Your sister is half Jew, and she's as pretty as they come. I don't have a thing against your mama, neither. Once I met her, she seemed like a regular person to me. Maybe not your daddy's type, but all right in her way. She paid those people at the Jewish place... what did you call it, David?"

"Jewish Children's Agency."

"She paid those people at the Jewish Children's Agency a lot of money to get a Jew child, so it makes sense that you come out like one."

I knew enough about Grandmama to know that she was insulting me. And my mother. I wanted to stand up for Jews to her, but for some reason I felt ashamed that she thought I was one. "All the Jewish kids at my school celebrate Christmas," I said. Which was true.

"They pray to our Lord Jesus?" she asked.

"Leave the kid alone," my father said.

I was liking this. Grandmama was making my father really nice.

"On Christmas Eve we go to church, and we sing hymns and everything," I said. "The whole school. Mom says her favorite part is when the music teacher sings 'O! Holy Night.'"

Grandmama just stared at me. She looked like a pitiful old lady. Almost as pitiful as my father had looked when he cried. But then she said, "If you're going to be a Jew, your inside needs to match your outside."

"My parents agree on religion," I said. "Me and Ada are nothing. And I like being nothing."

"Ada and I," my father said. For a second I didn't know what he was talking about. Then I remembered that he always corrected my English, no matter what. "Ada and I are nothing," I said.

Grandmama wasn't one to lose. "So when are we going over to see your sister?" She hardly ever called her by name. Grandmama believed her name was pronounced Ay-dah, like a friend of hers, and thought my parents were snooty for saying it any other way.

I looked at my father. I wasn't taking that question.

"Ada's very busy this time of year," he said, like he was all up on what Ada was doing.

"I'm here for two weeks," Grandmama said. "And I'm not getting any younger. You don't ask a child when she can come see her grandmother. You tell her."

"Ada doesn't want to see Dad anymore," I said. I don't know why, but I wasn't scared to say it. "She's almost eighteen. I think she can do that."

"You're supposed to respect your parents until you die," Grandmama said. "If your parents had sent you to Sunday school, you'd know that. They even teach you the Ten Commandments in Jew Sunday school. That's where everybody got them."

I wondered if those Ten Commandments said anything about hitting people. I really was feeling kind of brave. I never told on my friends, but I'd told on kids I thought deserved it. "Dad hits us."

I expected anything except for Grandmama to burst out laughing. She really was laughing, not faking or anything. "Davy Fisher hitting people? You've got to be kidding me. Your daddy was the biggest sissy I ever saw. And I know your mama isn't the type to put up with him hitting you. People like her believe in talking to kids. Spare the rod crap."

"He hits Mom, too."

She looked at my father for a fraction of a second. I could have sworn she had something like respect in her expression. Then she looked at me hard. "I dare you to tell me you ever saw that. The first time any man ever laid a hand on me, I'd have called the police before he even pulled back a stump where his hand was."

I didn't look down. I didn't look away. I just stared right back into her eyes. I'd never done that before. She sure had funny eyes. Brownish-yellowish.

"Elise annoys the hell out of me," my father said. "But I restrain myself. Don't listen to Otto. He's probably inherited his mother's creative streak."

I hoped Grandmama wouldn't jump in to remind him that I was adopted.

Grandmama pushed herself away from the table. "I'm not getting in the middle of this foolishness," she said. "Now somebody get me that girl on the phone."

I was happy to dial Ada's cell. I knew she wouldn't answer. And with a cell, there was no way to listen to a message until after it was finished. She couldn't pick up in the middle of it. She'd see my father's name come up and ignore it. But she'd sure check the message as soon as the call ended.

"Hey, it's Otto. If you get this, call me back here at..." I started to say "Dad's," but knew that would piss her off. I couldn't say "my father's." because he was listening, and I sure couldn't say "our father's." I looked at the phone, which of course had no number on it, then I asked my father what the number was.

"It shows up on her phone," he said.

"Call me back here," I said. "Grandmama wants to see you."

After I hung up, I waited a minute, but nothing happened. I knew very well that Ada had that phone on her at all times, probably even when she and Finn were fooling around, though I didn't like thinking about that. She wasn't calling back on purpose. I told Grandmama I guessed she didn't have her phone with her.

"I wasn't born yesterday," Grandmama said. "When you get home, you tell her to pick a day, any day. I'm free."

The reason Ada hadn't called back was that she didn't like surprises. "You can't throw something as huge as Grandmama at me and not let me think about it first," she said, and we both laughed. Grandmama was funny to look at, even if it wasn't funny to be around her. When we were little, she had seemed like the tallest person in the world, partly because our mother was so small, and partly because Grandmama was taller than our father and even outweighed him. Now that I was growing a lot, I could see that she was probably only about five-ten and under 200 pounds, but she didn't move like a lady at all. Kind of leading with her chin, if that makes sense. When she came into a room, she meant business.

Ada was dying to see Grandmama, as long as she didn't have to see Dad. I didn't understand, but she said I would if I came along. She'd drive, and we'd pick Grandmama up when my father was at Tulane. He was off work, but he said he had a lot of work to do in his office. Ada said that was probably a big fat lie. He just wanted to get away from his mother, and he knew she wouldn't be caught dead on a college campus. "She'd think people were looking at her funny," Ada said. "And they would be."

We pulled up in front of my father's house, and Ada had to admit that it was a cute house. Cute. The same thought I'd had, but I'd never said it out loud. I couldn't wait to tell him. He'd hate to hear it. I was dying for her to see inside, because inside was definitely not cute, but Ada said she was paranoid. I didn't have any idea what that meant. "It's bad enough sitting out here," she said.

"With my luck he'll come driving up and see me." I rang the bell for Grandmama, who took a good five minutes getting herself out of there. Ada was white with nerves by the time she came out. Ada had told me to open the front car door for Grandmama, and she plopped in backside first and didn't try to hug or kiss Ada. She wasn't that kind of grandmother, thank goodness.

We went out to Bozo's near the lake. I knew Ada too well. She always would ask the family to go there if we went out to dinner, and I knew it was because she figured nobody from Newman would see her out with her family, because nobody from Newman ever ate in Metairie, especially someplace like that. Grandmama's idea of fancy was Olive Garden, at least from what I could remember from her other visits. She didn't see any reason for my father to spend a couple hundred dollars taking us all out to a real New Orleans restaurant when she liked Olive Garden just fine. My mother would mumble that Olive Garden cost just as much as Galatoire's.

I loved Bozo's. Since I'd been little I'd believed the seafood had been in the lake only a few minutes before I ate it, and that made it good. I got the seafood platter, and Ada got fried oysters, and Grandmama looked at us like we were Chinese people eating dogs or something, and she ordered a well-done roast-beef sandwich on toast. "Dressed?" the waitress had asked, which everybody in New Orleans knew meant with lettuce, tomato, and mayonnaise, and she said, "Sure." When it came dressed, she told the waitress to take it back, that she only wanted mayonnaise. Even I knew what that waitress did with that sandwich, though if she'd been in the city, she'd probably have spit in it, too.

"Okay, girl, why aren't you talking to your daddy?" Grandmama asked, as soon as we had our drinks.

"You want the truth?" Ada asked.

"Better believe it."

"Because I hate him." She took a sip of her iced tea with her straw and looked right at Grandmama like she hadn't said anything very interesting.

"I don't want to hear talk like that."

She scared me to death. I could feel it all through my body, like in my blood. Ice. But Ada was past being scared. "You're the one who wanted to see me," she said, but she said it softly.

"So don't use words like 'hate.'"

"What about words like 'beat the crap out of'? He beat the crap out of us. That's why I dislike him extremely intensely."

"What's your mama say about that?" Grandmama said. "You've got two parents, you know."

"He beat the crap out of her, too."

For the first time ever, I saw Grandmama with nothing to say. Luckily, it was the peak of the lunch hour, and all the different lunch plates were already fixed in the kitchen, so our food came out fast, and she started eating that sandwich, which made her look busy while she was trying to think. Ada was scanning the room with a worried look, like someone she knew was going to pick this time to walk in and see her with me, which wasn't so bad, and this crazy old woman in a polyester dress with purple and pink flowers on it and the expression of a murderer on her face, which *was* bad. I couldn't believe I'd ordered the biggest thing on the menu, and it was all I could do to eat the catfish strips.

"Your parents need to get over this foolishness," Grandmama finally said. "I know your daddy, and he was never like that as long as he lived in my house. Matter of fact, he was so tenderhearted, I thought he might have been a homosexual. A boy would pick on him in school, he wouldn't hit back. I'd smack him, I mean smack him hard, and he wouldn't even put his hands up to protect himself. Sure wouldn't try to hit back.

"I'm not saying you got the best family in the world, but this mess you got, well, the solution sure isn't to have your poor daddy living in the ghetto while all of you are living in that beautiful house he's paying for."

Ada was sitting next to me, so I couldn't see what she was thinking, but I knew what I was thinking, and it was bad enough. When Ada didn't talk, I decided to say something. "You said the first time a man hit you, you'd call the police before he pulled back the stump where his hand was," I said to Grandmama.

She laughed. She sure loved her old self. She looked at Ada to see if Ada was laughing, but no sound was coming from her at all. "You hear the word 'first' in there?" Grandmama said. "I said the first time a man hit me he'd be a goner. From what I get from you two, and either you're in cahoots or you're telling the truth, your mama and daddy have been in the ring together more than one time. Am I right?"

We both nodded. We'd forgotten that our mother once said that there was no point ever trying to reason with Grandmama, and we should never try.

Grandmama let Ada pick up the check. Mom had given her cash because she expected that to happen.

After we dropped her off, Ada said to me, "Well,

that was kind of stupid." I waited to find out why. I had a million reasons, but they probably weren't the same as hers. "I was hoping she'd get so mad at your father that she'd go back and tear him to pieces. She's probably proud he finally grew a pair."

I knew what she meant by "grew a pair," and I thought that was a disgusting way of talking about my father. But only because of who he was. Anyway, I asked her what she thought Grandmama was going to do instead.

"Oh, she'll wait for him to come home, and she'll say stuff like, 'What do you think you're doing, hitting women?' But she'll say it like she's saying, 'What do you think you're doing, stealing ten million dollars from the bank and then running off to the Bahamas and getting away with it?' Kind of proud, you know?"

"You think she'll tell him to get back with Mom?"

"You heard her. Definitely. That's why this was so stupid. You'd think the woman would be glad he was rid of his 'Jew' wife."

"I miss him," I said. "I know you don't, but I do. He's my only father."

"He's my only father, too, but sometimes nothing's better than something bad. You need to think about that."

Before we went on Mardi Gras break, the seventh grade had learned about Sadie Hawkins Day. We'd never heard about it before because it came only once every four years, when February had twenty-nine days, and the last time we'd only been in third grade, when we didn't care about that kind of thing very much. All we'd learned was

Leap Year. Now we had to have a dance, which meant girls had to ask boys, and no boys could decide whether it was a mark of honor to be asked or not to be asked. I was kind of thinking I had a win-win plan, that a girl would ask me, and then I'd say my grandmother was in town from South Carolina and I couldn't go. But then a girl asked me, and my grandmother from South Carolina demanded that I refuse, and it got all mixed up.

The girl was Samantha Rivers.

She called me at home Monday night. She didn't sound scared to be calling a boy, the way I'd have been scared calling a girl. I was completely surprised. "Hey, I want to take you to the Sadie Hawkins Day dance Friday night," she said.

"Are you crazy?" I said before I could think.

Samantha laughed. That was pretty great, I had to admit. You'd have thought that snooty Samantha Rivers would have hung up in my ear. I started laughing, too. "Boy, I don't know where that came from," I said. "I totally apologize."

"So you'll go?"

I had to think fast. It was like when somebody throws you a ball and says, "Think fast." My plan was to tell any girl that Grandmama was in town, and I couldn't go out that night. But I'd already hurt Samantha's feelings once. Well, I hadn't hurt her feelings, but I hadn't been nice. "My grandmama's in town from South Carolina," I said. "She probably wants to see me Friday night. Can I call you right back?" I could call Ren. Maybe I could call Grandmama. Maybe I could call Ada. Maybe I could ask Mom. Maybe I could think.

Samantha told me she really needed to know that

night. I was only thirteen, but I knew what that meant. She probably had a list of other boys. In fact, she probably had a list with names higher than mine that she'd already called. But all the boys were from our class. She should have known we were all going to ask each other in P.E. class. Definitely, I'd call Ren first. But I told her I'd have an answer before 8:30. That was totally fair.

Ren said everybody knew Samantha was going to call me first. Even Nate, who liked her. So how come nobody told me? Because that's not fair, he said. Fair to who? I asked. Ren said he didn't have a clue. Geez, this was our first dance. All he knew was that this was something good, and I shouldn't be a jerk.

"But Samantha is the biggest jerk in the class," I said. "If you can call a girl a jerk."

"Did she act like a jerk on the phone?"

I had to admit that she hadn't. "So maybe that's what this is all about," Ren said. I knew what he was saying, but I didn't know what he was saying. I didn't bother to call anybody else. It was only 7:30, but I waited until almost 8:30 to call her back. I didn't want Samantha to know it mattered.

I got voice mail. I hung up. Voice mail made me really nervous. Especially in a situation like that. I could just see Samantha not checking messages and thinking I hadn't called and calling somebody else and me being considered an asshole and then me trying to say, *But I left a message,* and Samantha telling all the girls not to ask me, and then I'd be ruined even though I never wanted to go to begin with.

I dialed again, and Samantha answered on the first

ring. "Wow, I'm so glad you called back," she said. "I saw you on caller ID."

I told her it was all cool with my grandmother, and she told me that she and her mother would pick me up at seven on Friday. Her mother? I didn't say anything out loud, but it hadn't occurred to me that I was going on this date with her mother, too. Maybe Samantha was going to change one day, but Mrs. Rivers was never going to change. Mrs. Rivers always walked around acting like she'd won something. Having me in her car was not going to be her idea of having a prize. I just hoped this wasn't going to be one of those school activities where parents stayed the whole time. But there was no way to ask Samantha.

February 29 was actually on a Wednesday, so the party was going to be on March 2. Which meant that I was going out to eat with my father and grandmother on the actual Sadie Hawkins Day, and Grandmama was making a big deal in the car about how it was her treat. I rode in the backseat and listened while my father insisted on going somewhere inexpensive like Wendy's, which didn't do the trick. Grandmama didn't think he was being thoughtful about her money. She thought he was insulting her and calling her cheap. I leaned forward, taking it all in. My father was trying to come up with places I knew were cheap, but that Grandmama wouldn't because she didn't live here. Riccobono's. She'd eaten there. Who needs breakfast for dinner? How about Five Happiness? You see any cats around the dumpsters at

PATTY FRIEDMANN

Chinese restaurants? No, you do not. Ever wonder why? Cheesecake Bistro? She liked the sound of that all right. "I think I've got self-cleaning arteries," she said, and that settled that. My mother would have said, "You can eat at Galatoire's for the same price." To my mother, Galatoire's was the gold standard. To my Grandmama Fisher, Galatoire's was a lot of linen tablecloths and women in $500 dresses.

"We're having a Sadie Hawkins dance Friday," I said once we were seated at the table. My father wanted to know when. I told him.

"You can't go," he said.

"A girl already asked me."

"She'll have to unask you," he said.

That absolutely wasn't possible. For starters, I'd already told Samantha I'd cleared it with my grandmother. But that was just the first thing. I couldn't back out for any reason. Even if she was a real pain in the butt, Samantha was kind of considered the hottest girl in my class, and I had no clue why she'd asked me to the dance. It wasn't because other boys had turned her down, since Ren had said I was her first choice. And Ren would have told me if it was on a dare. I had to believe she wanted me for her date. And if I wormed out, I'd be considered a total jerk for the rest of seventh grade and all of eighth grade. And then we'd all go off to different high schools, and the word would get around the entire city that Otto Fisher surely hated girls because he messed over Samantha Rivers in seventh grade, so don't go out with him.

"You don't get it," I said. "This is the coolest girl in my entire grade."

My father looked like he was trying to remember back to his one experience with the kids in my class. "The only one I remember is that girl whose family came over on the Mayflower," he said. "And a girl like that isn't going to talk to somebody who gets up there and says his name is Shebsel. Shebsel! Mama, can you believe my kid got up in front of the entire school and said he was descended from some guy named Shebsel?"

Grandmama let out a good chuckle that made her kind of bounce. Why did he remember poor Shebsel's name? I wanted to blurt out that Shebsel died in a concentration camp, but my mother once told me Grandmama was a Holocaust denier and never to mention the Jews in World War II to her. She'd explained that Grandmama didn't believe six million Jews were killed by the Nazis, and I should never discuss it with her because I'd hate her.

"Miss Worthington asked Shebsel to the dance, and Shebsel was her first choice," I said.

"Well, Shebsel needs to spend Friday night with his grandmother, who is leaving Saturday morning," my father said.

"If you hadn't moved out, I could see her when I get home after the party."

"My moving out is not my fault," my father said.

"But you moving back could be your decision," I said.

"This kid is smarter than you give him credit for," Grandmama said.

The nice thing would have been to offer to be picked up or dropped off at my father's house before or after the dance. But there was no way on earth that I was going to have Mrs. Rivers see that one of my parents lived in a part of town where she would never go in the daytime, let alone at night. So I just kept saying I couldn't come on Friday night, and my father just kept saying I had to call Miss Worthington to cancel, and finally Grandmama got sick of it to the point where she probably didn't care if she ever saw me again, ever, and she said it was perfectly all right if maybe I just rode with them to the airport Saturday morning. The flight was at 9:20, which meant she wanted to be there at 7:30, which meant they'd pick me up at 6:45, but it beat fighting, and it definitely beat backing out on Samantha.

I thought maybe when I was rattling around the house on Saturday morning in the dark that I could tell my mother I wouldn't need to be doing it if my father still lived there. She wouldn't have to think about just having had Grandmama visit for two weeks.

CHAPTER TEN

Samantha rang the doorbell exactly on the minute. I was in the living room waiting, even though Ada had told me that you were supposed to be in your room still getting ready when your date came. At least that's what girls did. She'd quit doing that a long time ago, of course, since she didn't have anything to prove to Finn.

Samantha had a little flower in her hand. She looked really pretty, I had to admit. She'd done something with her hair that she'd never done for anything before, not even for her own birthday parties, like it had sort of a wave in it, and it stood out from her head, with a ribbon in it that matched her dress. I could feel my mother watching from the kitchen. "Here," Samantha said, and she handed the flower to me. It was all wrapped at the bottom with tape and had a pin in it. *Oh, I got it.* Men wore those on their jackets at weddings.

"Oh, crap," I said, "I didn't get you flowers." We were still standing in the doorway.

My mother popped out, like a superhero or something, come to save me, but she didn't say anything.

"My mother says I'm supposed to bring you flowers because I asked you to the dance," Samantha said. "Here, give me."

She pinned that thing on me like she'd been practicing. I was glad I was wearing a jacket, because it would have looked terrible if I'd just been wearing a shirt and vest, like I'd planned. "I have to get a photo," my mother said.

"Oh, crap," I whispered to Samantha, and she giggled.

"My mom's in the car," she whispered back.

That made me nervous. My mother's foolishness was going to piss off Mrs. Rivers. I'd seen Mrs. Rivers get pissed off. It wasn't pretty. If she got out of her car and started hollering, I'd have to give up. Give up what, I didn't know, but I'd have to give up.

Thank goodness my mother had come out of the kitchen locked and loaded. Her camera was on, she shot six frames in half a minute, didn't ask us what we thought, and we were out the door. I could see Mrs. Rivers in the dashboard light of her Mercedes GL550, which seemed to me to be a lot of car for a family with just one kid. She was fiddling with her cell phone, like she didn't care what we did. Thank goodness I wasn't at my father's house. It was possible to get carjacked with a Benz like that in any neighborhood in New Orleans, but Mrs. Rivers would be sure it would happen in his.

I opened the front passenger door for Samantha, and she said, No, her mother was going to chauffeur us, that we could both ride in the back seat, so I opened the door behind it, and Samantha scooted in.

"A girl is not supposed to slide over," Mrs. Rivers said. "You're supposed to just sit there and let Otto go around." No *Hello, Otto,* no nothing. I sat there with my hands in my lap and figured this was going to be my longest ride to school ever, even longer than on test days. I didn't know why, but I thought about that pig named Maxwell in the Geico commercials that kept squealing, "Weeeee, weeeee, weeeee!" while the mom driving just rolled her eyes. That's probably the way Mrs. Rivers was thinking about me. I started smiling and turned toward Samantha. "You ever see that commercial with the pig named Maxwell?"

Samantha just started laughing. That commercial hadn't been on for a while, but it didn't matter. You could just think of it and laugh. "What's so funny?" Mrs. Rivers called from the front seat.

Samantha made herself stop laughing. "Never mind."

"Don't be rude."

"Sorry."

I whispered, "Maybe I should explain?"

Samantha whispered back. "Just stay quiet."

"So, Otto, I've heard of your mother, but what does your father do?" Mrs. Rivers asked.

I'd been in school with her kid my whole life. That was a weird question. To anyone else I'd have just said that he taught English. To her I said that he was a professor at Tulane. "I didn't see him tonight," she said.

I looked at Samantha. I thought maybe her mother had made her ask me to the dance so she could find out if my parents were divorced or something. "We were there for, like, one minute, Mom. His sister wasn't there, either."

I couldn't believe it. Samantha was all right. It might

have been that she actually wanted to turn out nice, and I was her way of doing it.

The dance was in the gym. In honor of Coach, everybody had to take their shoes off at the door and go in socks or stockings or bare feet. Samantha took my shoes and hers and put them in a corner away from the rest because she said she wanted to be able to escape. I got nervous. I hoped she didn't want to go outside and kiss me. I'd never kissed a girl. For all I knew, Samantha had kissed a lot of boys. Though nobody had said anything. Not even Nate, who probably still had a crush on her, but never did anything about it. Samantha might have gone to Sunday school or something and met older boys there.

Ada had been wrong about the party. She'd said that as soon as everybody got there, the girls would go on one side of the room, and the boys would go on the other side, and the whole point of having dates would be over with until it was time to get our rides to go home. I didn't know about everybody else, but I thought being at school with a girl was weird and interesting, and I wanted to try it out, and I didn't walk up to my friends unless Samantha was next to me and their dates were next to them. Of course, we didn't have anything to say, but that made it weird and interesting. Samantha was probably the best date, because she could talk basketball. She knew about the Hornets, and she knew how to play the game, and she'd ask a boy what position he played, and eventually his date would look pissed at her, and I'd say I was thirsty or something.

The music was loud, and a lot of people got out and looked like they were dancing. I had an older sister, so I really knew how to dance, but when Samantha and I got out on the dance floor and I could tell she didn't have a clue, I quit fast. That's when she asked if we could get our shoes and go outside. And that's when I got scared. Good scared, but scared.

It was cold out, and I was freezing because I was so nervous. We sat on the steps that led up to the fourth-grade classrooms, so at least we were out of the wind a little. I was shivering, even though I had a jacket, but Samantha seemed okay in just a sweater.

"You want to know why I asked you to the dance?" she asked.

"Actually, not really," I said, and I laughed to let her know I was kidding.

"What do we have in common?" she said.

I tried to think. Absolutely nothing. I couldn't think of one thing. If you put the seventh grade up on a chart, any kind of chart, Samantha and I would be on opposite ends. "We're opposites," I said. "Does that count?"

She thought about it. "A little bit," she said, "but only tangentially." That proved it. What kind of person, thirteen or otherwise, used words like that?

"I know you're going to think this is crazy, but I think you're the only person who'd understand. I hate my mother."

I hated her mother, too, but I wasn't going to tell her that.

"She's not my real mother."

"Oh!" I got it.

"See? Everybody thinks my life is so totally perfect, but it totally sucks."

I told her I got that, but that anybody would get that. I wasn't really the best person, because my life wasn't perfect at all.

She kind of leaned into me, and it was a loving kind of lean, and I didn't mind at all. "That's my whole point," she said. "You've got a choice to go looking for your real parents, and so do I. Don't you ever tell your mom, 'You're not my real mother?'"

My birth mother had never crossed my mind. At least not in the present. I'd thought about how she hadn't had the little stuff that was me poisoned out of her thirteen years ago, but it never occurred to me to picture her as a person now. I loved my mother. I pretty much loved my father, too.

I told Samantha I'd never said anything about my "real" mother except that she'd let me live.

Samantha reminded me that her birth mother had named her, which meant she'd been sad to say goodbye. Then she reminded me that her adopted mother was a bitch. I tried not to nod in agreement. "You think I like doing everything right all the time? I can't ever mess up. I mean, I'm scared my hair is going to grow out darker. Or that I'm going to get an A minus. She doesn't see me as a person. I'm just something to show off. Like she bought me."

"My father sure wishes he'd gotten you instead of me," I said. I wasn't ever going to forget him at the Thanksgiving program. One thing about Samantha: no Jewish person was sitting in her family tree.

"Aw, come on, he's still got you, doesn't he?"

I had to think about that one. At least I could say he'd kept me for thirteen years.

"Pretty much," I said.

"My mother tells me all the time that I'm damn lucky I got adopted into a rich family, and the least I can do is show my gratitude."

"Wow, she *is* a bitch." The second the words were out, I slapped my hand over my mouth. But Samantha grinned, then leaned over and kissed the hand that was covering my mouth. That was the way I got my first kiss from a girl.

I held hands with Samantha in the car on the way home and squealed, "Weee, weee, weee," and said, "Next time I'll get a pinwheel," and we just laughed and didn't care. It wasn't like we were boyfriend and girlfriend, just friends, both free in some kind of way. When I got out of the car, I said, "Thanks, Mrs. R.," just like Maxwell did in the commercial, and Samantha was doubled over in a laughing fit when they pulled off. Mrs. Rivers didn't even wait to see if I got inside safely, and it was almost ten o'clock.

I felt all cold on the outside and warm on the inside, and I burst into the house hoping somebody would be around to hear about my evening. I thought it would say something about my family, compared to Samantha's family, and lucky for me, my mother and Ada and even Finn were all there, all excited for me.

"Did you kiss her?" Ada said.

"So what if I did?" I said.

"Your father will wet his pants if he finds out your

girlfriend is a descendant of the people who came over on the Mayflower," my mother said. She sounded really sarcastic.

"Hey, I was really happy," I said. "Don't kill my buzz."

"You women need to chill," Finn said. "You're like buzzards circling."

I told him thanks. I needed to think. Samantha had made me think, but so far my thinking hadn't made sense. I knew I wasn't jealous of her anymore. I even wasn't sorry to be me anymore. By that, I mean that it was all right not to be all A pluses and it definitely was all right not to be all blond and gentile-looking the way Grandmama Fisher thought people should look. Hell, Grandmama didn't like the way my father looked, and he'd had blond hair when he was a kid. Besides, I looked a little Jewish, which a lot of people outside my family said was going to make me look like a male model when I grew up. Any boy who cared what he looked like was gay or an asshole. But not both.

My thinking was all over the place. I'd definitely gone to the party with no Adderall in my system. What had Samantha said? Oh, right, that my parents still had me. They'd never told me I was lucky to be in a rich family, well, in their family, which might not have a Benz, but it had a famous mother and a professor father, which was just as important, maybe. So all it needed was to get back together, and my father would still have me.

"Dad needs to come back home," I said.

"Where'd that come from?" my mother said.

As best I could, I explained how Samantha and I both were adopted, and Samantha was like some fancy electronic device her mother had bought to show off, and she hated that, and she said I was lucky, that my family still had me, just the me that I was, so I needed my dad to come home and keep me.

My mother had a cup of tea that was getting cold in front of her. She drank it down. "Maybe it's important for Otto's sake," she said to Ada.

"You want Otto's sake?" Ada asked. "You want Otto's sake?" She turned to me. "Listen, you don't get me, do you?"

I thought I did get her. She hated my father because he was mean. That was good enough for me.

"You don't know half of it," she said. "When you know what I know, it'll be a different story."

"Aw, come on," my mother said. "You've promised to keep all that quiet. Once he knows, it'll ruin how he feels."

"Well, you've got to tell me now," I said.

No matter what my mother would have said, Ada was going to tell me anyway. If not right away, then as soon as she got me alone. My mother covered her face with her hands. So much for coming home all happy about Samantha.

"You ever ask yourself why you even got adopted in the first place?" Ada asked.

"Because they couldn't have another kid."

"Know why they couldn't have another kid?" She didn't wait for me to answer. "Because when I was three, Mama got pregnant. And you know what? Your dear father didn't want any more kids. Apparently, I was more than he wanted. Or maybe just enough, if I flatter myself.

"Anyway, he made her get an abortion. We're talking go-to-the-doctor-and-get-all-scraped-out."

"Do I have to hear this?" I asked. I didn't want to know about my mother's private parts.

"Sorry," Ada said. "So then Mama got really depressed. I mean, like she could barely take care of me. Or do her art, which meant she didn't make very much money. I don't know which bothered him more. Probably the money.

"So he decided he'd better do something or Mama wasn't ever going to be normal again, so he said he'd changed his mind. Sort of a deal that if she'd forget he made her have the abortion, he'd let her have a kid. Trouble was, she couldn't get pregnant. Maybe she was too old, or maybe, well, you probably don't want to hear this, but I think the abortion messed her body up, okay?

"They couldn't exactly say, 'Oh, well, too bad,' so they decided to adopt, and the only place where it was easy was at the Jewish agency because, you know, there just aren't as many Jews as everything else. And I guess they got approved pretty easily, which to me means they were dying to give away babies, because if I worked there I never would have given that man a baby. Remember how one time I told you that when they came to our house I told the lady I had head lice and that the kitchen was full of cockroaches, because I thought she'd get the idea that this was a terrible place for a baby? But she told Mama right in front of me that I was jealous after being an only child? We got poor you, anyway. I was only six, but I did my best.

"He told those people he'd raise you Jewish. That probably was the smallest lie he told. I mean, he probably said he liked kids. I bet Mama believed him as much as the social worker."

So far I didn't see anything that my father had done wrong except force my mother into an abortion, which was really mean, but otherwise I wouldn't have been adopted.

"Okay," Ada said, "this is what I'll never forget for as long as I live. You were what Mama called the baby from hell. I guess that was ADHD from the outset. I mean, whizzing around your crib the day you came from the hospital. You couldn't eat right, you couldn't sleep, you cried all the time."

"This isn't making me feel good."

"I loved you to death," Ada said. "You were my darling boy. I wouldn't put you down every second I was home, unless Mama made me do my homework. And she carried you like a papoose."

And?

Ada took a deep breath. My mother sat up straight. Her eyes were wide. I knew my life was about to change.

"And when you were six months old, your father sat Mama and me down and said he wanted to take you back to the agency. You were a tiny baby, an adorable baby, a baby named Otto, and he wanted to take you back. He was serious. Of course, Mama said no, and I screamed bloody murder, and Mama said he'd made a deal with her.

"He said big effing deal, but he didn't say effing, and he picked you up and grabbed a box of diapers, and he had you all the way into his car, which of course didn't have a car seat, and he was going to take you back to the agency. He meant it. Mama was fighting with him, right there by the car, and I was standing there hitting at him, and if that lady Mrs. Eugene, who's got a kid at your school now, hadn't driven by and stopped and asked what was going on, there's no telling what would've happened. If he'd taken you down there to that agency like that, they probably would have taken you back."

She looked into my eyes the way people always did when they wanted to be sure that ADHD wasn't in the way and I was going to hear nothing else but what they said next.

"It's time to start over, Otto, it's time to start over."

I was going to start over, all right. Just not the way Ada wanted me to.

ACKNOWLEDGMENTS

Thanks to Victoria Brownworth, who with one email squeezed this book from my desiccated brain. And huge gratitude to Bob Jeanfreau, who knows why.

ABOUT THE AUTHOR

Patty Friedmann's first young adult novel was *Taken Away*, which was a finalist for ForeWord Small Press Book of the Year in 2011. She is also the author of six darkly comic literary novels set in New Orleans: *The Exact Image of Mother*, *Eleanor Rushing*, *Odds*, *Secondhand Smoke*, *Side Effects*, and *A Little Bit Ruined*, as well as the humor book *Too Smart to Be Rich* and the literary e-novel *Too Jewish*. Her novels have been selected for Discover Great New Writers, Original Voices, and Book Sense 76, and her humor book was syndicated by the New York Times. Her reviews, essays, and short stories have appeared in *Publishers Weekly*, *Newsweek*, *Oxford American*, *Speakeasy*, *Horn Gallery*, *Short Story*, *LA LIT*, *Brightleaf*, *New Orleans Review*, and *The Times-Picayune* and in the anthologies *The Great New American Writers Cookbook*, *Above Ground*, *Christmas Stories from Louisiana*, *My New Orleans*, *New Orleans Noir*, and *Life in the Wake*. Her stage pieces have been part of *Native Tongues*. Recently *Oxford American* listed *Secondhand Smoke* with 29 other books that included *Gone With the Wind*, *Deliverance*, and *A Lesson Before Dying* as the greatest Underrated Southern Books. With slight interruptions for education and natural disasters, she always has lived in New Orleans.

other books from

Tiny Satchel Press

www.tinysatchelpress.com

Taken Away

a novel
by Patty Friedmann

Taken Away by Patty Friedmann

It's the last week of August 2005, and Hurricane Katrina is about to hit the Gulf Coast—hard. As the storm comes closer and threatens to destroy New Orleans, 15-year-old Summer "Sumbie" Elmwood's two-year-old sister Amalia undergoes open-heart surgery. She survives the surgery, but when New Orleans is evacuated, Amalia disappears from the hospital. With the city deserted and destroyed and no food, water, electricity, or phone service available, the Elmwoods are forced to leave New Orleans without Amalia and go to Houston to stay with Sumbie's aunt. The FBI and others search for her missing sister, but thousands are missing and the little girl is no one's priority. Sumbie's parents begin to suspect that Sumbie did something to Amalia. With the aid of two would-be boyfriends, Hadyn and Robert, Sumbie tries to find her missing sister and prove her innocence in the chaos left by the killer storm. Will she succeed? Or will she become the FBI's prime suspect?

"Patty Friedmann is one of the finest writers in Louisiana. Not only did she stay in New Orleans throughout Hurricane Katrina and its aftermath, she ended up being rescued twice! No one knows New Orleans better and no one is better qualified to write about that period."—Julie Smith, Edgar Award-winning mystery author

ISBN 978-0-9845318-2-0

The Secrets of Loon Lake by J. D. Shaw

Sarah Ramsey's summer at Loon Lake won't be like any of the other summers spent at the isolated lake where her parents grew up. Sarah's parents are barely speaking and her pretty and popular older sister is getting all the attention.

Sarah enlists her two best friends, Jake and Rob, on an excursion to the forbidden Big Island. There they discover a pile of old bones in tattered clothes half-buried near a small bungalow. Jake and Rob don't want trouble, but Sarah's curiosity won't let it go. She begins to investigate and uncovers another mystery: a hotel that burned down in the 1920s, killing several people. A fire that was no accident.

In an era of cell phones and Internet access, Sarah has to dig through old newspapers and talk to the great-grandmother of neighbors to glean facts. The revelations stir up something evil. Sarah is threatened, her sister mysteriously disappears, and Sarah must find answers before something terrible happens.

ISBN 978-0-9845318-0-6

Leave No Footprints by **J.D. Shaw**

It's the middle of the night when Beth Watson sneaks out of the house, steals a car, and drives, desperate to run from what she's seen, from what happened to Jack. She drives until she ends up in a sleepy little Michigan resort town as the summer season draws to a close. All Beth wants is to escape, stay unnoticed, fly under the radar. But tiny Beaumont is a town with big secrets, and Beth arrives at the same time that a murderer strikes.

Beth, who has never gone to school, never held a job, and isn't even sure if 16 is her real age, enlists the help of Dee, the town's café owner, who sees a little of herself in Beth. Beth finds herself in a world she's never known—a world of other teens, cell phones and computers, cliques and bullying, girlfriends and boyfriends. And killing. So much killing. When the murderer strikes again and again, Beth is certain her plans to start a new life are over—and the worst is yet to come.

"*Leave No Footprints* is a deftly drawn portrait of a young woman who just wants to be normal—if only she can escape her past, which is a mystery even to herself."—Joanne Dahme, author of *Tombstone Tea* and *Contagion*

ISBN 978-0-9845318-6-8

Sorceress by Greg Herren

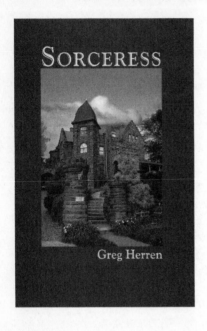

Seventeen-year-old Laura Pryce has just completed her junior year of high school. Her parents were killed in a car accident weeks earlier, and she is moving from Kansas to California to live with her great aunt Melisande LaValliere, whom she has never met. Sad and depressed, Laura finds herself drawn to Jake, Melisande's handsome young handyman, himself the victim of a horrible family tragedy.

Melisande's estate is huge, and Laura can't help but notice there are a number of paintings of women who look just like her hanging on the walls, each from different periods in history. Melisande explains that a genetic quirk leads to a girl in each generation being born with the "LaValliere face," which leads to a wholly unpredictable life, including visions.

Laura finds herself having nightmares about magical rituals and reliving episodes from the lives of the LaValliere women whose portraits hang in Melisande's house. When Jake begins to share her visions of these ancestresses, Laura begins to question where to turn and just what moving to her great aunt's home might cost her…

"*Sorceress* is a delightfully creepy thrill ride. Filled with twists and turns, it will have you jumping at every bump in the night and leave you afraid to close your eyes."—Michael Thomas Ford, winner of the American Library Association Award for Young Adult Fiction

ISBN 978-0-9845318-1-3

Immortal Longings by Diane DeKelb-Rittenhouse

Lauren and Kayla are the perfect high school couple–except they aren't actually a couple. Smart and sarcastic Lauren is secretly in love with her best friend, Kayla, one of the most popular girls at school, who changes partners (male and female) like other girls change shoes.

One autumn afternoon, the two 17-year-olds wander into Manhattan's newest vintage clothing store, Deja Nous, and agree to take after-school jobs at the enticing shop. On the ride home to Queens, Kayla talks non-stop about the wonderful clothes, how much fun she and Lauren will have working together, and the store's the intriguing and beautiful owner, Elizabeth Valiant.

Deja Nous soon becomes an obsession for the teens, but it isn't until Lauren starts putting together the puzzle pieces of the Valiant family and recent events that she realizes that she and her beloved Kayla are in danger from a centuries-old curse. Will Lauren be strong enough to save them both, or will the power of forces she never imagined be stronger than her love for Kayla?

ISBN 978-0-9845318-4-4

From Where We Sit:
Black Writers Write Black Youth

Black Writers Write Black Youth
edited by Victoria A. Brownworth

Thirteen established and emerging African-American writers present a range of compelling and provocative stories in this exciting collection, with a wide range of dynamic characters, divergent styles, and compelling issues. Jewelle Gomez, acclaimed author of *The Gilda Stories*, offers a new episode in her historic series. Harlem native and award-winning writer Mecca Jamilah Sullivan, romance writer Anne Shade, short-story stylist Craig L. Gidney, actress and playwright Ifalade Ta'Shia Asanti, noted children's author Becky Birtha, and award-winning novelist Fiona Lewis each explore what it means to be black in America today as well as in America's historic past, addressing issues not only of race, but also of class, gender, sexual orientation, and religion. Filmmaker Lowell Boston details the multi-faceted complexities of racism in America for young black men, while emerging writers Lisa R. Nelson, Guillaume Stewart, Misty Sol, kahlil almustafa, and Quincy Scott Jones take on different aspects of urban life: Nelson presents a young girl who wants to escape her middle-class neighborhood, Stewart writes provocatively about missing fathers in black America, Sol explores the impact of gun violence and no-snitch rules, almustafa details the day-to-day suspicion young black men face, and Jones places a young black man in white academe in a dazzling display of wordplay.

ISBN 978-0-9845318-3-7

Dreaming in Color by **Fiona Lewis**

Carlene—her friends call her Cee-Cee—came to the U.S. from Jamaica to be reunited with her mother, who has been working to make enough money to send for her. But for Cee-Cee, life in her new country is hard. She misses her island home, the friends she left behind who don't even Facebook her anymore.

High school is a minefield of bullying. It's not even October and talk of homecoming and parties has Cee-Cee super depressed after the boy she likes plays an ugly trick on her. When a group of mean kids, led by one of the most popular girls in the school, targets Cee-Cee, taunting her for her accent, she turns to art as a refuge.

Then Cee-Cee meets Greg, another teen from Jamaica, who plays saxophone and has his own secrets. Greg and Cee-Cee stand up to the bullies, but then events take a devastating turn.

"Fiona Lewis grabs a handful of issues in her new novel and tosses them back out on the table with sensitivity, wisdom and clear-eyed vision. And you can't put the book down!"—Jewelle Gomez, award-winning author of The Gilda Stories

ISBN 978-0-9845318-5-1